This book is for everyone
who enjoys a good story
about "ghoulies and ghosties
and long-leggety beasties and things
that go bump in the night. . . ."

Fawcett Crest Books
by Norah Lofts:

THE GOLDEN FLEECE

THE BRITTLE GLASS

JASSY

TO SEE A FINE LADY

THE LUTE PLAYER

ELEANOR THE QUEEN

WINTER HARVEST

SCENT OF CLOVES

HEAVEN IN YOUR HAND

BRIDE OF MOAT HOUSE

THE LITTLE WAX DOLL

THE TOWN HOUSE

THE HOUSE AT OLD VINE

THE HOUSE AT SUNSET

THE CONCUBINE

HOW FAR TO BETHLEHEM?

THE LOST QUEEN

THE KING'S PLEASURE

LOVERS ALL UNTRUE

A ROSE FOR VIRTUE

OUT OF THE DARK

NETHERGATE

CROWN OF ALOES

KNIGHT'S ACRE

THE HOMECOMING

HAUNTINGS

HAUNTINGS

Is There Anybody There?

BY NORAH LOFTS

A FAWCETT CREST BOOK

Fawcett Books, Greenwich, Connecticut

CONTENTS

"Is there anybody there?" said the Traveller,
    Knocking on the moonlit door;
And his horse in the silence champed the grasses
    Of the forest's ferny floor:
And a bird flew up out of the turret,
    Above the Traveller's head:
And he smote upon the door again a second time;
    "Is there anybody there?" he said.

But only a host of phantom listeners
    That dwelt in the lone house then
Stood listening in the quiet of the moonlight
    To that voice from the world of men:
Stood thronging the faint moonbeams on the dark stair,
    That goes down to the empty hall,
Hearkening in an air stirred and shaken
    By the lonely Traveller's call.

Extract from "The Listeners" by Walter de la Mare

Note

Have you ever noticed how often, when the company is congenial and the night ages, the subject of haunting will crop up, and how many apparently hard-headed people have had some eerie experience?

Any ghost story finds in me a ready customer, though I prefer something less concrete than ladies in grey draperies and gentlemen in buff coats. And naturally with my obsession about houses I find the idea of a haunted house extremely attractive, in theory, if not in practice. I would avoid one with only the slightest dubious reputation as I would the plague.

In my day I have been a great house-hunter, not only

for myself, for friends, even strangers. Advice to house-hunters who do not wish to share a home with something unseen. . . . Pretend otherwise, say wistfully that the place would be perfect if only . . . Out will come the story of something on the stairs, the door that opens of its own accord, the room that is always cold. Then take to your heels. If no such story is forthcoming, propose a second inspection, and take a dog. Dogs have a keen perception of the uncanny.

I don't claim to be psychic; I have never seen, never wish to see, anything or anybody who isn't there, but I am responsive to atmosphere and once, at a moment when I thought—Something odd! my dog companion, a stolid, very brave dachshund, suddenly screamed and fled. Oddly enough, when later, I took him to the notorious Borley Rectory, he showed no reaction at all; and in fact the Society for Psychical Research has since done a de-bunking job on Borley.

Despite a life-time's interest in hauntings, I have evolved no theory, nor adhered to one. I have a kind of general belief that places make an impression on people, and that people, in certain circumstances, can leave an impression on places. And the whole thing is still a mystery. In the most ordinary living-room, in an empty room, even, the essence of what makes for the BBC News is *there,* vision and sound, just waiting for the right contact to be made. A chest-of-drawers can make no such contact; a TV set can and does; yet it only records what has been there all along. I am inclined to think that much the same thing applies to psychic experience; certain people, in certain circumstances, become plugged in, switched on.

I very much hope that anyone attracted by the title

and the subject of this book will not suffer disappointment by the lack of grey ladies, buff-coated gentlemen, screaming skulls, bloodstains that no amount of scrubbing can remove. For me the essence of a good ghost story, like the essence of the horror story, should lie in what lurks behind the ordinary, often pleasant façade. All these stories concern pretty ordinary people in pretty ordinary circumstances; where houses are concerned they are not even necessarily old; certainly not the long-empty places, given over to bats and spiders and legends.

As I said, for this kind of story-swapping, the company should be congenial. Let us, for half an hour, be congenial, and ask—expecting no answer—Is there anybody there?

NORAH LOFTS

Mr. Edward

If I'd been in the habit of bothering God about trivial, material things, I should have said that Miss Gould's suggestion came as an answer to prayer. Ever since the Easter holiday I had been worried about the long one in the summer. When Tom died and I found a post as school matron and David went to boarding school, my father had said that we must spend all holidays with him. At first, though dull, they were pleasant enough; but as David grew older Father grew more critical, making outspoken remarks about the behaviour of the young nowadays and accusing me of spoiling. I confess I am inclined to be indulgent during the holidays; David's school is pretty Spartan, I don't see him often, and I am very fond of him.

During the last Easter holiday Father said to me, not for the first time, "You always were a born fool!" David threw down the book he had seemed to be engrossed in, went red in the face, clenched his fists, and said, "Don't you speak to my mother like that!" Father took hold of his stick and for a dreadful moment I thought they would come to blows. They're both at a silly age; Father seventy, David thirteen.

Miss Gould said that she realised that she was asking a great favour. I and everyone else on the staff know that this phrase often prefaces some preposterous imposition: she might easily be about to ask that I give up my holiday altogether. So what she said was a pleasant surprise. Some relative of hers had left her a house which she intended to modernise thoroughly and use, first as a place for holidays and then to make her home when she retired. She had already arranged for work to begin, and had then received an invitation to go abroad. She wondered whether I'd go and supervise the workmen. With difficulty I concealed my joy. Free lodging for eight weeks, our fares paid, ten pounds a week to spend on food and frivolity, my son to myself, and a cast-iron excuse to offer Father. My cup was full.

It overflowed when I saw the house. It stood in the centre of a pretty, unspoiled village, behind a high ribbon wall of red brick. Between wall and house was a sizeable garden, lawn, rosebeds, a wide herbaceous border. The house was early Georgian, very attractive, the red brick glowing between climbing roses and clematis. For the first time in four years I should be an ordinary woman, in a house temporarily my own, with my son for company.

The workmen, all cheerful and pleasant, arrived and got busy. The whole house was to be rewired, redecorated and the kitchen refitted; so there was an element of camping about our lives which added zest. Having meals at odd times and in odd places makes food taste better, and on this holiday I could afford good food and indulge David's carnivorous tastes. It was wonderful.

I had one small niggling fear, though fear is too strong a word, really; I was a little afraid that when the novelty had worn off David would be bored during the day. I took my duty to Miss Gould seriously and never left the house for long while the men were at work. They had their instructions, I had Miss Gould's scribbled lists and it was up to me to see that no mistake occurred. So I was free only in the evenings. However, by the end of the week, David had found a friend, the way boys do; another only son, home for the holidays and craving companionship. Paul had a pony and a swimming pool and very hospitable parents. Together the boys discovered the pleasure of brass-rubbing and ranged far and wide on their bicycles. David's days were fully and happily occupied.

We'd been in the house just eleven days when, on the point of departure in the morning, David said,

"Oh, by the way, I shan't be back for supper. It's Paul's birthday and they've asked me to stay for dinner."

I said, "How nice for you." Then, remembering

social obligations and the way boys could ignore them, I mentioned the advisability of taking Paul a present.

"I've got it," David said, and put his hand to his pocket. "I won't show you, because I know you don't like them. It's a fossilised f-r-o-g. Very rare. I swapped a good stamp for it."

I said, "I hope Paul will appreciate it."

That afternoon, as usual, the workmen knocked off at half-past five and silence fell. I dislike noise and on every previous day this had been a moment that I welcomed, no clatter, nobody in my way as I went about the preparation of the evening meal. That day it was different; the silence had a positive, oppressive quality; altogether too quiet. And I was alone in the house. Alone in the house for the first time.

Being alone had never bothered me; I'd been alone, slept alone in a number of places in my time. I positively enjoyed solitude. But here there was something different. First of all I noticed the deadly quiet, then I realised that I was alone, and then I had the fantastic idea that I was being watched. I ignored the feeling. I went about the house, tidying things up, closing windows, doing the things I always did, but I could not rid myself of that sensation of being followed, of being closely observed. It was hateful. There was something else too, I began to feel sad, self-pitying. As a rule, I can truly say, I'm not that; I'm lucky to have a job which I can do and which brings in enough to buy David's clothes and equipment and pay the bit of school fee that his scholarship doesn't quite cover; I'm lucky to have David, to be strong and healthy. I'm a widow; I miss Tom dreadfully, but as a rule I don't *brood.* Now it was as though all my deprivations, and shifts and petty economies were being exposed to a very sharp, pitying eye. It was most peculiar. . . .

I decided that I'd wash my hair, a job calculated to dispel any fanciful notions, for, for the last four years, to save time and money I'd worn it long.

I washed it very thoroughly, rubbing away as though by cleaning the outside of my head I could rid the inside of megrims. To an extent I succeeded, and presently, with a towel over my shoulders and my hair spread out, I went and sat in the sunshine that poured in through a window that faced west. I had a book and was almost lost in the story, when I had again that fidgety feeling of being watched. I did my best to ignore it. Then a startling thing happened. My hair was touched. It felt as though a hand had lifted some of it at the back, weighted it, let it fall, and stroked it. I jumped up and stood there, coming out in goose-pimples, but trying to give myself some rational explanation. A lock of hair had been caught up when I gave my head its first towelling, and fallen down as it began to dry. But I didn't believe that. The touch had been slow, lingering, a lover's touch. And it wasn't my memory playing tricks. Nobody had ever handled my hair that way, for as a child, a young woman, a wife, I'd always worn it short. I looked at the curtain, asking myself was it possible that a gust of breeze had made it sway out far enough to reach me. It was not possible. Panic took hold of me; I ceased to be able to think at all. I must get out.

I rushed into the garden, bright with flowers and sunshine, and stood there, shaking as though I had just had a narrow escape from some tangible danger, feeling nothing but relief. Then, gradually, I began to see myself as a fool, standing there with half-dried hair spread over a damp towel, having run away, from what? It would be hours before David came home; and there was nowhere that I could go; apart from the people at the shop and the post office, the man who delivered the milk, nobody in the village knew of my existence. The only thing to do, the only sensible thing to do was to go back into the house, pin up my hair, and make a cup of tea.

I couldn't do it. I looked at the house, so pretty, so almost prim in its symmetry, and knew that I couldn't enter it alone. Part of my mind scrabbled desperately for a fingerhold on sanity; I told myself that in the garden I could move around and stay in the sun and at the same time do a useful job. I went to the tool-shed and got a pair of secateurs and cut off masses of dead roses. The patches of sunshine grew smaller until the whole garden was in shadow, the long summer dusk set in. It turned cooler. Soon the only way to keep warm woud be to walk, and to walk round and round and round a garden seemed to be an admission of lunacy. So I alibied myself again. I'd go and meet David.

I knew where Paul lived, David had pointed out the imposing gateway when we had passed it in the bus on our way to the cinema in Whepford. It was about three miles out of the village. The dusk was not yet deep enough to allow me to walk along the street with a towel over my shoulders, so I removed it and left it in the garden. My hair I pushed back and left hanging in a style unsuitable to my age but not positively outrageous.

Actually I saw no-one; the only place where there seemed to be any life about was in the pub at the top of the street; that was brightly lighted and from it came the reassuring sound of human voices. I'd have given anything to be able to go in, speak casually to someone, have a heartening drink; but I hadn't a penny on me, I was a stranger, and my appearance was unlikely to gain me any credit. I had a sudden, very vivid impression of what it must feel like to be a tramp, or a displaced person. There is a loss of all identity. It takes a stronger personality than mine to assert itself in a vacuum, wrenched from its background, deprived of possessions, cut off from contact.

I reached my destination far too early, of course. Not that I knew the exact time, for I had removed my watch before washing my hair. We take for granted the ability to measure our lives into hours and minutes and the loss of it contributed to my feeling of not being real. Still, my state was only temporary, eventually David would arrive and life would be resumed. I sat on a bank, in the shelter of the massive stone gatepost and waited, until at last there was a sound of tyres on gravel and a wobbling light.

I made a great effort to act normally. I stood up and said, "David! It's me. Mum."

Startled, he swerved, said, "What the hell!" braked, and dismounted.

"What the . . . on earth are you doing here?" he demanded. "Is anything the matter?"

"Of course not. I just came to meet you."

"So now we can both walk home! What a witless thing to do!"

Ordinarily I don't object to being talked to as though

I were Smith minor; it argues a sound, healthy relationship; but I was cold and still shaken by my experience.

"There's nothing to prevent you riding home if you wish," I said stiffly.

"I didn't mean that," he said. "I wouldn't want to."

We began to walk in silence and then I had those thoughts that are so undermining to parental discipline; how little time David and I had together, how swiftly time passed, how soon he'd be grown up, pursuing a life of his own. . . .

"Nice party?" I asked, holding out the olive branch. He responded and we talked for the rest of the way. Not quite in our usual manner, though; a little self-consciously.

The house, when we entered it, seemed absolutely ordinary. My flight now appeared to be the unreal thing, something I'd dreamed or read about. David noticed my hair for the first time, looked at it with disfavour and said he hoped I wasn't going in for *that* fashion. He was right, of course, but I disliked his arrogant tone and went to bed remembering some of my father's remarks about widow's only sons and the necessity of cracking down now and then.

All in all I expected to have a bad night, but as soon as I was in bed I fell into a deep sleep of exhaustion, and slept until eight o'clock. The sun was bright behind the curtains and the scent of roses was strong in the room. I ran down in a dressing-gown to open the doors for the workmen, put on the coffee, and then went back to dress.

On my dressing-table lay a rose, one of my favorite

kind, a dark red one, so freshly cut that the dew still glittered on the velvety, half-open petals.

I thought—How like a boy! Die rather than apologise, and then make such a gesture. I found a pin and when I was dressed, fastened the rose to the front of my frock.

When David was on his second sausage I said, carefully offhand,

"Thank you for the rose. It's beautiful."

"What rose?"

"This one." I touched it.

"Why thank *me?*" He sounded gruff. Had I done wrong to mention it?

"Well," I said, "I couldn't just ignore it, could I? It was a nice gesture."

"I don't know anything about it," he said.

We looked at each other. In his face there was no sign of teasing, nor of what my father called slipperiness.

I said, "Oh, David, come now. Who else could have put this rose on my dressing-table?"

His stare shifted to the flower.

"It's wet. The whole garden must be wet. You can look at my shoes *and* my slippers, if you can't believe me."

I did believe him; I was speaking to myself, rather than to him when I said,

"Then who did?" Who did?

He underwent one of those startling changes possible only in a literate teen-ager with a jackdaw mind that collects and hoards information of every kind.

"You could have done it yourself. Subconsciously of course. Like shoplifters who're really giving themselves presents. Women like presents, specially flowers. And you've got nobody but me, and I didn't think of it. So you got it for yourself. Without realising."

I just managed to say,

"Then I must have been sleep-walking."

He looked at me with interest.

"That's possible, too. You could tell by your shoes." Then he reverted to boy again and tackled his third sausage.

I unpinned the rose and put it on the table. It lay there, lovely, awful, a question mark. I knew that I should never again like dark roses: I knew that I must place myself between the thing I suspected and my innocent, sausage-eating son. I took a long drink of coffee and asked, "What are your plans for today?"

My own day, outwardly moving in routine, was spent in mental confusion. One moment I'd give way to credulous weakness and think that there was something uncanny about this house; that a disembodied hand had caressed my hair, that the rose was what they call an apport. From that I'd leap away in fright and seek refuge in David's explanation about my own subconscious mind. It was *just* possible that having so much given I craved more and supplied it myself. The fondling touch on my hair could have been the long-term result of a thought I'd entertained once or twice when my hair first began to grow and to ripple and curl. I had thought then what a pity it was that Tom had never seen it that way. But the truth was that I was really no more at home with such terms than I was with the thought of psychic manifestation. I hated the thought that my own mind could play me such tricks; that I, too, was at a silly age.

David's plans for the day had been a little vague and had included the possibility that he and Paul would go to the cinema and afterwards sample the food at a newly opened Chinese Restaurant in Whepford. So all that day there ran through my speculative confusion the near-certainty that I should be alone in the house for some time after the workmen left. I took precautions; I placed a chair and a rug in the garden; I ate my makeshift meal early. When the men left I was tempted to go straight out, sit in the chair, and wait for David's return; but it seemed *silly*. The end of all my thinking had been that, whatever the cause, my panic of yesterday had been unjustified. It was simply fear of the unknown. I'd behaved just as the Mexican Indians had behaved when first confronted by harmless horses. Inexplicable things weren't necessarily frightening. And to go and sit out in the garden would be to *admit* . . .

So at half-past five I went and sat down, in the sitting-room, to mend David's sweater. The door of the room and the door of the hall I had left open, cautious, and despising myself for being cautious.

I darned diligently for perhaps ten minutes before feeling myself under observation. The feeling grew and I became uncomfortable, though, forcing myself to be calm, to be reasonable, I could feel that there was nothing unfriendly about this observation. It was, actually, rather like being watched by a dog which hopes to be taken for a walk or given something, yearning, wistful, very intent. I bit the inside of my cheek; I told myself that I wasn't frightened.

I'd come to the end of one bit of mending and reached for the scissors. My hand had almost closed

on them when it was arrested. The sensation was quite
indescribable. I wasn't paralysed, but I couldn't move.
There I was, with my hand stuck out at an angle,
hovering over the scissors; exactly as though someone,
fond of me, had taken it and said, "That's enough
for now. Pay a little attention to me!"

There slipped into my mind a third possibility, almost too delicate to be entertained, but a thing I must
face. Could it be Tom? Once, when my grief was raw
a sympathetic friend had tried to woo me to spiritualism,
and I'd been repelled by the vagueness, the in-
coherencies, the sheer banality of the procedure. But
now there slipped into my mind the possibility that
here, in the first place where I'd been happy and at
ease since his going, the time might be ripe. . . .
After all, the touch on my hair had been a caress; the
rose designed to please. Perhaps something was needed
of me; some effort. Perhaps I was on the brink of
some astounding revelation.

I thought of Tom, concentrating fiercely. Then,
aware of temerity, I spoke his name, softly.

Instantly my hand was released, flung back at me,
and the quality of the watchfulness changed, perceptible
as a change in temperature. Never, in all my life, had
I been the object of such hostility. Truly frightened
now, I staggered to my feet and went blundering out
into the garden, making, not for my carefully-prepared
chair, but for the gate. I'd almost reached it when
David came swooping in, riding one-handedly and
clutching a parcel to his chest.

I was past pretence; for a moment I couldn't even
speak. Fortunately he attributed my state to surprise
at seeing him. He hastened to assure me that there

was no sinister reason for his early return. It was
simply that they'd discovered that the film being shown
that day was one they'd seen, so they'd postponed
their outing. And he'd thought that there'd be nothing
much for supper, so when he'd seen a mobile fish and
chip shop . . . He was so overcome by his own fore-
thought and resourcefulness that he was unobservant.
I managed to say,

"What a splendid idea!"

He pushed his bicycle into the half-ruined conservatory which stood at the side of the house, and
which served as cycle shed and store for the workmen's
materials; then together we went into the house, and
when I had reheated the food and warmed the plates
we sat down to what could have been, but for my
preoccupation, a merry meal.

The problem was, what to do now. I was certain—or
as certain as one can ever be upon such a debatable
subject—that there was something badly wrong about
this house. My instinct was to get away at once. Get
away? Ruin David's holiday? Offend Miss Gould past
all hope of forgiveness? Forfeit that generous board
money? Or stay? Stay and be terrified?

I tried to think rationally about being frightened.
Fright speeded the circulation, poured adrenalin into
the blood. It made people perform feats of which
otherwise they were incapable; one form of it, stage-
fright, was responsible for some outstanding perfor-
mances. Only with people whose hearts were already
weak could it do actual harm. I was strong.

And again, what was I frightened of? Apart from
being frightened of being frightened. I could not recall,

offhand, any instance of a disembodied entity inflicting physical injury.

Sitting there, snug in the kitchen, with the homely scent of fish and chips in the air, I told myself that I had nothing to fear but fear. But I'd take care, I thought, to avoid being in the house alone.

That was on Wednesday, and the rest of that week was so easy, so uneventful, that complacency set in. Face a problem boldly, I thought, and it solves itself. Even the business of being in the house by myself was no bother; on the day when David and Paul went to the cinema two of the men worked late. Paul spent a day with us and stayed until he was fetched at ten o'clock; his parents invited me and David to dine with them in circumstances of great splendour. On the other afternoons David was home before the workmen left. Also, at the back of my mind was the cheering thought that even a haunted place was not necessarily haunted all the time; such things had their cycles. Or perhaps whatever it was that had tried to oust me—the spirit of some old Gould, long dead, who objected to the alterations, and held me responsible—had sensed my determination not to be ousted, and given up. Oh, I was full of soothing theories.

On Sunday the weather broke; dark bruise-coloured clouds hung low and there was intermittent rain. David and I had planned an outing, but we abandoned it. He spent most of the day mounting his brass-rubbings, and I wrote several letters, one of them my weekly report to Miss Gould.

At seven o'clock in the evening I went towards the kitchen, intending to make a salad. The kitchen was reached from the hall by a short, cupboard-lined passage, dim at any time, and now almost dark. I reached for the switch, which had been on the left-hand side; then I remembered that here the rewiring was complete and the switch was now on the right. Before I could touch it I was seized, there is no other word for it. The forceful pressure which had arrested my hand when I reached for the scissors was now applied to the whole of me; I was stopped, clasped, almost lifted from my feet. And helpless. In a second I knew I should be breathless, the pressure was so great. I used my last gasp to shout.

David came, galloping and slithering. By the time he was there, the switch pressed and the passage lighted, I'd been released, flung against the wall, only just conscious enough to be aware of his face, paper-white, eyes wide with alarm. It took the greatest effort of my life to say,

"I twisted my ankle."

Testy from relief, he said,

"Well, what d'you expect? Running about in the dark?"

Gently, but with surprising strength, he heaved me into the kitchen and on to a stool, and said he knew just what to do for a sprain.

"Not a proper sprain," I muttered, "just a twist."

But he had taken charge and I had to submit to the rough-and-ready treatment of the playing-field and the dressing-room. A tea-towel soaked in cold water was applied, and covered and held in place by a split plastic bag.

"Be as good as new tomorrow," the prefect told Smith minor in heartening tones. He then made the salad as competently as he had bandaged me, and throughout the meal kept the talk going with some grisly accounts of wrenched ligaments and broken collar bones, all designed, I realised, to make my accident seem unimportant. My response was not what it should have been, though I was not, as my son plainly thought, making much of a small injury. I was brooding over the fresh turn things had taken and wondering was it possible to stay on, to hold out, if the presence of another person in the house was no longer a safeguard. And I kept seeing myself explaining to Miss Gould that I simply couldn't stay in the house any longer. Could I offer her the real reason? What would be an acceptable alternative? Oh dear, how I envied whoever it was who merely had a broken bone, even if it did stick out at the unlikely angle which David was demonstrating.

That night I slept badly, little snatches of sleep, with alarming dreams, and long wakeful spells when I lay, wary as a hunted animal, working the treadmill of inconclusive thought. Once I dreamed that David shouted for me. We were now, through the dictates of the work's progress, sleeping in rooms with a communicating door. I put on my light and padded across, opened the door cautiously and peeped in. He seemed to be sound asleep, but he was uncovered, and the night, after the dull day, was cold. I tucked him in with a thought for the past, when he was small and I'd done it so often; and then I tensed, aware once again of being watched. I hurried back to bed and thought—I can't do it; I can't stand the strain. . . .

But morning came, and with it the sun, the cheerful

men; courage flickered again and cowardice absolutely flared when I thought of facing Miss Gould.

Over breakfast David asked,

"Did you come into my room last night?"

I said, "Yes. I covered you up. Everything was on the floor. And your window wide open."

"I thought you did," he said. "But I was too sleepy to speak. The funny thing is, I thought you *un*covered me."

"No, I covered you," I said, glad to have a fact to fasten upon, something I could say with certainty. Most of my mind was busy with its egocentric problem. I missed the significance. I wasn't warned.

Nor did I realise what I did when, two days later, I yelled for David again.

Because of the painting being done we were always opening and closing windows. In the room which was one day to be Miss Gould's drawing-room there were three, a french window that opened on to the lawn and on each side of it a sash window reaching from floor to ceiling. They'd all been painted that day and the men had said that it'd be safe to close them, with no fear of sticking, any time after eight.

I closed the french window first, latched and locked it. I went to the one on the right. It was heavy and I had a struggle with it. I thought—Really, I should have a pole for this job. And then, as I pushed, it was exactly as though someone, helpful, much stronger than I, came behind me and lent a hand. The window moved easily; and then I was seized, exactly as I had been in the passage outside the kitchen, but this time from the rear.

I shouted and David came. I was released.

I said, "The window . . . too heavy . . . you must help."

He shifted the paint-brush from his hand to his mouth, holding it between his teeth and mumbling over it,

"Was it all that urgent? I was just . . ."

He closed the window easily.

". . . on a tricky bit," he said.

I apologised for interrupting him. And I thought—Saved again. But I wondered how long I could go on, hopping as it were, from stepping stone to stepping stone.

On the following afternoon David decided to clean his bicycle and set to work, as soon as the conservatory was all his own, armed, amongst other things, with some substance guaranteed to restore chrome to its original brightness. Cooking in the kitchen I was near enough to hear some of his movements and his whistling. Suddenly there was an almighty crash, a mixture of dull thump and clanging metal. I dashed across the bit of paving between the kitchen door and the conservatory. The bicycle and David lay side by side on the floor; blood from his head was mingling with white paint from a large can, one of several that stood on a high shelf. For one ghastly minute I thought he was dead; but he wasn't. I knelt down beside him, lifted his head, found the wound, and applied pressure to it with my wadded-up apron. I am accustomed to emergencies and know that head-wounds bleed freely; but as the apron reddened and he did not regain consciousness, I lost my professional calm. I must get the doctor. The telephone was not yet installed; I must run to the post office, find out the name of the nearest doctor, and ring from there. Then, as I was rising from my knees I looked at the shelf from which the paint can had fallen. Fallen? David must have been standing on this side of the bicycle; the paint can, had it been subject to the ordinary laws of gravity, would have missed him by miles.

I daren't leave him, not even to call a doctor. The full awfulness of my situation, together with the recognition of my foolhardy obstinacy, struck me simultaneously and I broke down into helpless sobbing.

To give way completely can sometimes have a restorative effect. I braced up immediately. I could carry the boy, or failing that, drag him. I would not be beaten; I would not give in. But an insensible, well-grown thirteen-year-old body is not easily handled, and this one, in places, was slippery with wet paint. Still, my struggle was not without result.

David came to; I felt the change. Under my hands the inert, badly stuffed sack became a human frame again.

"Whassa matter?" he asked in a drunken way. "Whadda you trying to do?"

"Get you to a doctor."

"Whaffor?"

"You've had a little accident," I said. "Could you walk just a step or two?"

"Walk a mile."

I helped him up, told him to put an arm over my shoulder, put my arm around him, and we set off, reeling towards the gate. There we were lucky. A passing motorist, whose name I never knew, though I shall never forget the look on his face when he saw us, slowed down. Halted.

To my babble about getting to a doctor he replied, "Casualty, I think," and drove us rapidly to the hospital at Whepford, where David had six stitches put in his head and was given the routine anti-tetanus injection. Then, because his speech was still slurred and his movement badly co-ordinated, they said there might be a slight concussion and it would be as well to find a bed and keep him under observation. They told me, very kindly, that there was nothing to worry about and that I could go home.

I found a deserted waiting-room and spent the night there. In circumstances calculated to induce insomnia in the Seven Sleepers of Ephesus, I made my plans. They were governed, as most ordinary people's plans are, by economics. In that house, which David must never enter again, which I myself should enter most unwillingly, was contained, not merely my own modest, expendable wardrobe, but David's school trunk and everything it contained, all those things which must be provided in triplicate and marked with Cash's name tapes. For me a salvage operation was imperative.

The Sister in charge of the ward where David lay said,

"You're early!" and gave me a look which denounced all parents as neurotics. She forbad me entry, because patients were being washed. But she said that David had slept well and asked for egg and bacon for breakfast. He'd be seen at about ten o'clock, and if I came back or better still telephoned, after that, I should be told whether he was fit for discharge, and if so, at what time.

I took the first bus back to the village.

The house was full of workmen when I arrived; I

explained that my son had had an accident and was in hospital and that I intended to take him to the seaside to recuperate as soon as he was discharged, making that event sound unpredictable and distant. They were sympathetic, and I traded on their sympathy, gladly accepting help with the trunk, with my own suitcase, the labelling of the bicycle. The can of paint, the horrid mixture of scummed white paint and blood evoked a comment from someone, supposedly out of my hearing, "The young bastard must have been fooling about in here." I let it pass.

At ten o'clock I was in the post office. I telephoned a car hire firm in Whepford, and then the hospital. David could be collected at my convenience. I dispatched an expensive, explanatory telegram to Miss Gould. Then I went back to the house.

The old man who kept the garden in order was at work on the herbaceous border. It was the first time that I had actually seen him, though the state of the garden testified to his erratic ministrations. Once he had come, worked, and departed while I was dealing with the vast amount of dirty laundry David had brought back from the school; another time he had come, worked, and departed while we were spending the evening with Paul's parents. I felt, in the circumstances, that I should go across and have a word with him.

He was incredibly ancient; the pupils of his eyes had a milky rim, and he had no teeth. I imagined that he had lost his own, and his gums had hardened into efficiency so long before the National Health Service was installed that he had felt no need for the use of it. The toothlessness gave his enunciation a curious sibilance.

He was inquisitive about Miss Gould, whom he had only seen once, and not, I gathered, in her most genial mood.

"If she's one to want a younger man," he said darkly, "then she'll hev her work cut out." Young men didn't go looking for jobs these days; too well paid. Man and boy he'd worked in this garden seventy years come September, and when he started he'd earned six shillings a week. And when, as he sometimes would, Mr. Edward gave him half a crown, he'd felt like a millionaire. The name triggered something in his memory, his eyes took on the old-man-remembering look.

"Ah. He was a one, Mr. Edward was. Wild as they come, but with a nice way to him, if you know what I mean. And what a one for the ladies!" His milky old eye brightened, the sibilant voice had relish in it. "You wouldn't remember," he said, with tact, "but there was maids in them days. And the funny thing was, even a right plain girl'd look pretty, dressed like they did, specially of an afternoon, black and white, you know. First time I see my own missus in her outgoing clothes I was daunted." He seemed about to digress, but recovered his theme and went on. "It's got so his Ma wouldn't hire a girl under forty, not less she'd got a squint eye or some such. But I always liked him, scandalous or not. And what happened to him was a shame."

"What happened to him?"

"Oh, he went to the War. Boer War that was. Long afore your time. There was horses then you know. He looked fine when he went off, Mr. Edward did." There was an element of hero-worship in the old man's voice. "And he come home on a stretcher. Shot through his spine and helpless as a baby. He didn't linger long. It must hev been hard on him. One nurse he had was a right goodlooker." He gave a gentle sigh, said, "But this ain't getting nowhere," and bent to his work again.

It had got me somewhere. There is a theory that places generally admitted to have something uncanny about them have been associated with some violent emotion, fear, remorse, or revenge. Lust is an emotion too. In this house it had been strong, I could just imagine those parlourmaids, willing, unwilling, coy, flattered, so pretty in their afternoon black and white. I could imagine the frustration that had been hard during the short lingering time . . .

I looked at the old man, placidly working, and I thought that I could tell him more about Mr. Edward than he could tell me. When rebuffed he turned nasty; he was pathologically jealous; a dangerous as well as a scandalous character.

I went to the door and asked the men who were burning and scraping the grained varnish from the stairway if they'd mind bringing out the trunk and my case. I was careful not to step across the threshold.

Victorian Echo

When my great-aunt Julia died she was eighty-seven, and she had attained her last objective, which was to die in her own house.

She left far more money than anyone would have expected. Most of it went to rather obscure charities, but she left her house, its contents, and a thousand pounds to me; a surprise and a very pleasant one. She had always lived very parsimoniously; I had sometimes wondered if she had enough to eat and on my visits had taken food, making rather thin excuses.

Joe and I went out to look at my inheritance on a Sunday, the only day on which we were both free. It

was mid-March, a sunny, windy, hopeful day with cat-
kins in the hedges and primroses in the ditches. Joe did
not know the house well; he had come with me a time
or two, but Julia disliked him and showed it.

The house was unique, the remnant of a much larger
one damaged by fire some time around 1800. Its rooms
were few, but spacious, with pleasing features. It was
incredibly cluttered, since Julia had hoarded everything,
even old newspapers.

I groaned. "What on earth am I going to do with it?"

"I'll help," Joe said. "Some of this," he blew gently
upon a feather boa, "might be useful to the Amateur
Dramatic Society. And I'll bring some boys along to
clear the real rubbish. Don't you worry."

Joe wasn't only my husband, he was my friend.

The tour of inspection over, I said: "Well, what shall
I get for it?"

"A couple of thousand. If you're lucky."

"So little? Oh, surely, Joe. Look at the little old cot-
tages where you can't stand upright. They make three,
sometimes four thousand."

"Look at the plumbing here. Look at the wiring.
Look at the kitchen."

"I know; but at least it is on the mains. And it is well
built and has some attractions."

"Well, you'll know when it's valued for probate. To
my mind it's a bit of a white elephant."

Then he said: "How about living in it ourselves?"

More of a surprise even than the legacy.

We had been singularly lucky when we moved into
this district in finding a house to rent. A house, more-
over, which was only ten minutes' walk from the library

where I worked and about fifteen minutes by car from the school in which Joe taught. It was a small house, semi-detached, but it stood in a pleasant little cul-de-sac and the idea of moving had never occurred to me.

I said: "That needs thinking about. It might mean two cars." Our hours, our free time, even our holidays seldom coincided. "And I had *thought,* well, maybe it was silly of me, but I thought at least four thousand, to put away, a little nest-egg against the time when I shall have to stop working."

My doctor had just confirmed my suspicion that I was pregnant; and they can yap-yap-yap away all they like about equality; the fact must be faced. A man can go to work, if needs be, on the day his child is born; his wife cannot. And afterwards there is a time when a baby's best friend is its mother.

Joe said, in a way so unlike him, so violent, so almost vicious: "Yes, I know. The day will come when you can't go dishing out mush about doctors in love with nurses."

That astounded me; and so did my answer to it.

"A public library," I said haughtily, "serves many other purposes, as you well know. Any job can be made to sound silly. Even drumming vulgar fractions into little blockheads."

I stopped, appalled. Joe and I had had many arguments; what married couple have not? Never before, so far as I could remember, had we said things specifically designed to *hurt.* But I thought that going over a house crammed with things that had outlasted their owners was a dreary business and had affected our nerves.

I said: "I am going to get some daffodils. Coming?"

Joe said: "No. I'll take another look at those prints.

You may be more of an *heiress* than you think." He put his hand on the knob of the door of the room which, years before either of us were born, had been the sanctum of my great-uncle Alfred, who'd died in 1913.

The garden had been under-cared for four years. "Four shillings an hour," Aunt Julia had said of her gardener on about my first visit; "how can anyone afford it?" Presently it was five and she could only afford it, she said, once a week, for one hour. But the tough and the willing things had survived and I had hardly ever gone away after visiting her without an armful of something lovely.

I gathered a bunch of lovely white daffodils. Over my head there were the tight little grape-coloured buds that would be lilac, the tight pale candles in green holders of the chestnut tree. As I gathered the daffodils I thought that here Joe might take to gardening and get some much-needed fresh air.

I went into the house and I said: "Darling, I have thought it over. It would be lovely to live here. Let's do it."

"Not if you want four thousand for it." He looked at me as though I had demanded that sum, had held my hand out for it. He said: "If I'd taken myself into industry, by this time I could have supported my wife and given four thousand pounds for a house. As it is, the best I can offer is fifteen hundred."

He sounded so angry, so hostile. And what came over me? I was every bit as bad. I said, "Oh. And where would you get that?" Nasty, challenging voice.

"Cash in on my life insurance."

We went out, locked the door, got into the car, and

drove about a mile in silence. Then I said: "Joe." He
passed a dawdling car and said:

"Yes, honey?"

"It's *our* house, you know. We've always shared
everything, haven't we?"

We always had; even the washing up; even the business of whoever got home first lighting the fire and
getting the meal started. We had a joint account, either
signature valid on cheques. I don't think we'd ever had
a dispute about money in all our six years of married
life.

Now Joe said: "Yes. Of course. I just felt narked suddenly."

I thought—me too!

Nothing more was said about cashing in his policy.
Our preparations for moving went smoothly. Joe disposed of a lot of rubbish. I went over when I could, but
I don't think we were alone in the house together until
the day we had the row about the bathroom.

Most of the house's contents were not of much value,
but six chairs which I thought quite hideous would
fetch, the valuer said, £100 each and I felt that that
justified me in planning new fixtures in the bathroom.
I went and chose them—a pleasant muted pink set—on
my free day and when I told Joe about them he simply
said: "Sounds nice."

I was scrubbing the kitchen table. Suddenly Joe, who
had been arranging his books in the room that had
been Alfred's, walked in and said truculently: "There's
absolutely nothing wrong with that bathroom, you
know."

"Oh Joe, there is. It's all so ugly and the bath is

disgusting. You said yourself that the plumbing was awful."

"I did not. I merely suggested that you should consider it before putting an insanely inflated value on the place. The bathroom is perfectly adequate for anyone who wants a bath, not a narcissistic ritual, surrounded by pink porcelain and mirror glass."

He said that to *me,* who can take a bath in five minutes flat.

I said: "Anyway, I've ordered the stuff now."

"Inconsistent," he said. "One minute you're talking about saving a nest-egg. The next you go throwing money about."

I had an almost irresistible impulse to retort that it was *my* money; but I forced that back and held my tongue.

I said, "Well, I can't cancel it now."

"Then I will; if you're afraid of a plumber."

Really I could have cried; he sounded so unlike himself, so utterly unfriendly. The day was ruined for me.

On the way home we made it up again.

Joe said: "You have the pink stuff if you want it, darling. It was just, well, I felt the old bathroom was in keeping with the rest of it."

I said: "And you were dead right. I went up and measured and that grim old bath is at least six inches longer than the biggest they make now. We'll stick with it." Joe is a tall man.

But even as I said it I had a curious thought. *Inside* that house we seemed to quarrel.

We moved in. And it was all beautiful; exceptionally fine weather; the rooms looking lovely, the furniture from our little house settling down beside what we had kept of Julia's. But *something*, oh, so difficult to describe, had happened to us. We were a bit like enemies who have made a truce and fear that one foot, one word wrong might make war again.

It did, over breakfast, on a Thursday morning. Joe said: "I shall be late tonight. I'm going to give Whiffle's accounts a look-over."

Whiffle was notorious; most of his enterprises were just on the shady side. He had never been to gaol yet, but one of his associates was serving three years.

I said: "Oh Joe, you don't want to have anything to do with that man. He can afford to hire an accountant."

"He happens to have hired me," Joe said, in that hostile voice.

"He's a crook. If you've had anything to do with his accounts, and been *paid*, you could easily get into trouble. It isn't as though we needed the money."

"Speak for yourself," Joe said. "You can afford to sneer at ten guineas for an evening's work. I am not yet in such a fortunate position."

The very words he chose when in the mood I called "nasty" were different from those he ordinarily chose. I suppose mine were, too; for I said: "Ten guineas an hour would be poor pay for getting involved in a scandal."

That evening I drove home; no meal to prepare. I made a cup of tea and went into the garden. I cut some poppies, the last of the lupins, the first of the delphiniums and made a flowerpiece of such beauty that to look at it, alone, almost hurt. I needed a really hard job, and it was to hand, the sorting out of a mass of papers old enough to deserve a look-over before being destroyed.

So it was that I came across *the* letter. Closely written, much underlined. It was dated September 10, 1899.

My dearest Julia—Your letter has caused me the *greatest* grief. I think the knowledge of its contents would kill your papa. We thought you happy; indeed I opened your letter in joyful anticipation of receiving some *good* news.

You must *abandon,* once and for ever, any thought of leaving Alfred. Think of the scandal! Marriage requires adjustment, often to circumstances much harsher than yours. You say that you quarrel, and always about money. Alfred's income is limited and Papa's settlement on you was very *generous.* I fear that you have failed in tact. I sympathise with Alfred's criticism of your extravagance over clothes. A trousseau such as you were given needed no replenishment for at least a year.

As for your proposal to install a bathroom, Alfred is correct in calling it absurd. It may be your *money* but the *house* is his and has been in his family for generations. Naturally he wishes no alterations and says that a hip bath is adequate. You must not mention *your* money or make a display of spending it. It would be *wise* and *kind* to choose, for Christmas, or your birthday, some inexpensive article, well within Alfred's means, and ask him to *give* it to you. This will enable him to feel that he is playing the man's part and *providing* for his wife. . . .

This letter, containing so much insight into human nature, had been written by my great-great-grandmother. I was proud to be of her breed.

And then I thought—Julia kept the letter but rejected the advice: she had insisted on the bathroom; she had bought all those hats and clothes and shoes. She had stopped spending only when Alfred died, in 1913. With her enemy dead she no longer needed her weapon. They must have been very unhappy together.

Then I had another thought which made my scalp prickle. I know it was a fantastic thought; incredible, perhaps, but the incredible is so often merely the thing that has not yet been properly explored. It was once incredible that some scene in Washington should come bouncing off a satellite to be visible in an English sitting-room. Was it any more incredible that in this house there had been a clash of wills and personalities so intense that it had left its mark on the very atmosphere?

A kind of haunting far more destructive than grey ladies: Alfred in Joe; then Julia in me.

I went into the kitchen and cut some sandwiches and filled a Thermos flask with Ovaltine—coffee after eight o'clock kept Joe awake. Then I sat down and waited, thinking and thinking; growing in a way more certain. Even that disputed bathroom *still* a bone of contention! Odd, to say the least. But what I had to face was the fact that Joe had no time for things that couldn't be proved by figures, or defined by formula. I was afraid he would laugh.

When he came in he looked tired. I always know. He'd got some school stuff with him and would have taken it through to Alfred's room; but I did not want him to go there.

"You sit down," I said. "Feast your eyes," I pointed to the flowers, "and pour the Ovaltine. I'll take these along."

I went and came back and sat beside him on the sofa.

"Nice," he said, biting into his sandwich. "My favourite kind." And then, abruptly, he said, "Well, you'll be pleased to know that you were right. The man's an absolute crook and I've washed my hands of him."

I said, in a quiet reasonable voice, "Now why should you say I'll be pleased to hear it? And in that tone of voice, Joe?"

"Everybody enjoys being able to say I told you so. What tone?"

"One we've used sometimes lately. Unfriendly." I included myself, for I had used it, too. "And it's always about money, either directly, or indirectly. Hadn't you noticed?"

Joe munched another sandwich, meditatively.

"Come to think of it, yes," he said. "As a matter of fact I never used to think about money until . . . D'you know, I can remember the very minute. Standing out there," he nodded towards the hall. "Talking about what the house would fetch. It hit me. I thought—Ten years' hard slog and, man, all you've got is a bit of life insurance. And then you said something about a nest-egg against the baby's arrival. . . .

"I don't say I think about it all the time, but I've never been completely free of it. That's why I thought that if Whiffle really was the old muddler he pretends to be I could maybe put him straight and earn a bit on the side. I'm sorry if I've sounded sour. Frustration, darling."

"What about me? I can't plead that, can I?"

"In your condition anything goes," he said with the old friendly grin. "Some ladies demand strawberries in December!"

"I have a much more interesting theory," I said,

lightly. "Read this." He did so. "What's this got to do with anything?"

"I think we may have inherited more than the house." I explained. And of course he laughed.

"That's what comes of handling too much romantic fiction," he said. "Still, I tell you what—next time I feel poor, I'll blame Alfred. And hope it works."

I said: "I'll keep a sharp lookout for Julia, too."

As a matter of fact they became a family joke. Joe could say: "Alfred wishes to point out that to leave the bathroom light on all night is somewhat extravagant." I could say: "Julia wonders if it would be possible to have an electric percolator for her birthday."

Nevertheless, in my heart I am sure that we had escaped from what could have been a very nasty, dangerous situation: and I often remember that if Alfred had not sent Joe out to earn a possible ten guineas, if Julia had not saved the letter while ignoring its good sense, that situation might well have grown worse.

In fact, I sometimes think that what Joe and I did that evening, over the sandwiches, was not so far removed from the mystical ceremony called exorcism. . . .

Pesticide

"And what about Jennie?" It was an old problem and the question made a kind of chorus through my life. My sister Angela was ten when I was born; my brother Bill, twelve, Margery almost fifteen. My mother had actually resumed work and I can imagine that my arrival caused her considerable inconvenience. Inconvenient—though far from unloved—I had remained; too young to share pastimes, interests, holidays; "a drag" as Angela had once said when Mother urged that she should take me on a picnic.

Now, in June, as I was recovering—rather slowly—from having my tonsils removed, both my parents,

archaeologists, were invited to join a "dig" in Turkey;
Angela was perfecting her Italian in Perugia; Bill was
doing a stint of good work with the Labrador Mission
and Margery's exact whereabouts were unknown. The
last communication was from Libya, where she had a
job as secretary-interpreter to a Dutchman who had a
firm in Tripoli. It was a postcard of some splendid
Roman ruin and it said, tersely, "Shall not be here long.
Will write." No letter had arrived; nobody worried. As
a family we were happy-go-lucky as well as cosmopoli-
tan. But even my parents jibbed at the idea of leaving
me alone in the house.

Several ideas were discussed and discarded for this
reason or that; and then Mother had an inspiration. "I
wonder if Effie could have her."

Until about five years before I was born Effie had
been the kingpin of our household. To me she was
merely legend; the maker of wonderful pancakes, the
knitter of two Fair Isle sweaters which had somehow
survived and been inherited by me; a singer of songs, a
teller of tales, the owner of a fox terrier named Whisky.
Mother often said, "Oh, if only Effie were still with
us . . ." or "When Effie was here . . ." But Effie had
taken a holiday in that area loosely defined as the Cots-
wolds, and there she had fallen in with a man named
Owen Jenkins who had his own market garden. "It
seemed just right for her," Mother said, "she was always a country girl at heart."

Now, pressing her argument, Mother said, "She
might be glad of a paying guest for a couple of months.
I somehow gather that money isn't too plentiful there."
So letters and then telegrams were exchanged; and off I
went to Cheltenham.

I felt that I knew Effie by sight because, like the pull-over, certain photographs had survived. The last one, taken just before she left us, had even been enlarged and framed. It showed my father, looking as though he had strayed into it by mistake, my mother looking as though rounding up the whole family had been a cow-boy job—as no doubt it was—Angela, Margery, Bill, and in the centre somebody who could have been Mother's younger, much better-dressed, better-groomed sister; short, rather plump, with fair curly hair. "That's Effie, holding Whisky," I had been told. (The story of the taking of this snapshot was somehow typical of our family. Not until they were lined up in position, did it strike anyone that a camera must be manned. So Mother had run out into the street and stopped the first passer-by. "He seemed a bit taken aback," she said, "but he made a good job of it, didn't he?")

There was nobody remotely resembling the Effie of my imagination, or of the photographs on the station platform. This did not dismay me. I was quite accus-tomed to waiting until someone remembered where I had been left. When an old woman came toward me with a purposeful tread I assumed as casual and inde-pendent air as I could manage, quite prepared to tell her that it was all right, I was just waiting for some-body. But she said, "Jennie? Jennie Bridges? I'm Effie." She kissed me, rather hurriedly, but warmly and then went to pick up the biggest of my suitcases. She looked so small, and the case was big and heavy; all the lighter ones we owned were already widely dispersed or about to go to Turkey by air: I said, "You mustn't carry that. A porter lifted it down for me and he's about somewhere." I had my two-shilling piece ready and looked around for the man. Effie said, "Oh no. That would be a wicked waste. And I'm used to carrying things. Can you manage the rest?" Bent over sideways and moving at a kind of stumbling trot, she set off and clutching the rest of my possessions to me I followed to where a man waited in a vehicle known as an estate car. He did not stir, I don't think he even looked round as Effie opened the door at the back and heaved in the big bag and the others. Then she went to the passenger door, opened it, and said, "This is Jennie. Jennie, this is Mr. Jenkins."

Ours is a haphazard household but we are mannerly, and my father, though he may sometimes not quite know whether he is in the twentieth century A.D or B.C., is one of the most courteous men in the world. I reached my hand out and said, "How do you do?" Mr. Jenkins said, "Get in. Did you shut that door fast?" Effie said, "Yes. I was careful." I could see where I should sit. The passenger seat in front bent over and allowed access to a narrow space and a seat behind. I began to scramble in; but Effie said, "No; you sit in front, you'll get a better view." Mr. Jenkins said, "Have we not wasted enough time?" I continued to scramble —rather more hastily; Effie took the front seat.

My view, though necessarily circumscribed, was still entrancing, the countryside so different from that around Cambridge. The road went up and down between green fields and every now and then there were clusters of houses, all grey stone, most of them with roses growing over them.

I said, "It is pretty."

Effie said, "Yes, it is reckoned so." Mr. Jenkins said

nothing though my remark had been framed to please him. It was *his* district and in Cambridge anyone who professed admiration for the architecture, or the Backs got an instant good mark.

I tried another tack. I said, "Everybody sent their love, Effie." That was one of the statements, true in essence, dubious in detail, which are common currency. Had Bill, Angela, Margery known that I was going to meet, in the flesh, the Effie they remembered so kindly they would certainly have sent their love. My father and mother had.

Effie said, "That was kind." Her husband said, "She is *Mrs. Jenkins.*"

I said, "I'm sorry."

After that nothing was said. In a few minutes we came to a grey wall and a gateway. Mr. Jenkins stopped; Effie got out hastily, opened the gate, held it, and shut it again. He drove on, past the entrance to the pretty little house and into an open garage. There he stopped. Effie joined us and hauled that horrid heavy case out. Mr. Jenkins got out of the car and said, "I will shut in the fowls."

I said to Effie, "I'll help you." And I did. It was further from the garage to the house door than from the station platform to the parked car. I said, "It would have been better if he had stopped here, just for a minute."

She said, "He has his ways. And he is a man who does not take kindly to changes."

I pondered this remark as we hauled my stuff upstairs into a rather starkly furnished little bedroom. There I said, bearing in mind Mr. Jenkins' behaviour up to this point, "Didn't he want me to come? You don't have to keep me, you know. I don't want to stay where I'm not welcome."

She said, "Oh, it is nothing of the sort. No, Jennie, you must not think like that. It is his way. He is a very quiet man." She made a little fluttering movement with her hands. "He will be needing his supper."

As I unpacked, delicious scents of cooking reached me. When Effie—I could not so easily transfer to *Mrs. Jenkins* in my mind—called me, I hurried down. The table was set for three. Mr. Jenkins sat there, a steaming plate before him. To one side was Effie's place with the tea-pot and cups; I sat down opposite and she put a poached egg on toast before me. She herself had toast only.

Apart from Mother's belief in the health-giving properties of oranges, apples, garlic, and parsley, nobody in our house took food very seriously and I did not envy Mr. Jenkins his steak, onions, peas, and potatoes, but the scent of his meal gave me an appetite for my own. I took up my knife and fork.

He said, "In this house grace is said. Lord bless this food for our use and us to Thy service. Amen." He then proceeded to eat and to drink in a manner that would not have been tolerated in our graceless household. After a minute or two the noise began to get on my nerves. Talk might mitigate it I thought; I said, "This is a delicious egg." Effie said, "From our own hens." The brevity of the response, the almost apologetic little glance she shot at her husband informed me that further attempts at conversation would be unwelcome, so I ate on in silence and took stock of my companions.

To a ten-year-old anybody over thirty looks old;

but Effie looked *ancient;* deep vertical lines above her nose, others from nostrils to mouth corners, and virtually no lips at all. Her skin and her hair looked much the same colour, a kind of buff; she wore her hair pulled straight back and pinned into a tight little knob at the back of her head. Her dress, close-necked and long-sleeved, was dark brown with a fleck of half-hearted yellow.

Mr. Jenkins looked considerably younger; his hair was black, his face red and brown. He was short, for a man, and thin. He had prominent ears and a very long upper lip, deeply grooved. The odd thing was that though I had seen a blown-up snapshot of Effie, and in the woman opposite me now could see no trace of resemblance, Mr. Jenkins, whose face I was now studying for the first time, seemed almost familiar. I thought—given a wig to hide those ears he would be almost good-looking.

He said, "If you have done. For what we have received may the Lord make us truly thankful. Amen." Then he looked at me and said, "You have other clothes?"

"Oh yes," I said. "Like the black sheep. Three bags fuls." Three bags, one heavy, and he hadn't moved a finger.

"Then you will oblige me," he said, "by not going about dressed like a boy while you are under my roof. I have some standing in this village."

I was wearing jeans and a shirt. I jumped up and showed him the zip at the side.

"I'm not dressed like a boy," I said. "Boys have flies, at the front."

He looked horrified. He said to Effie, "See to it," and went off.

Effie said, "You must not mind him, love; he has his own ideas. He is a very good man and goes by the Bible and there is something about men wearing women's clothes—or the other way round. It is displeasing to God."

"But who can decide? Chinese women always wore trousers."

She said, "Please, Jennie. Let's not argue. It gets nowhere."

She began to clear the table; I helped her and presently she said, "I had no chance to ask. How is everybody?"

I gave as lively an account as I could and Effie brightened. She even laughed over some of Margery's exploits. When she laughed I could just glimpse a resemblance to the girl in the photograph and that reminded me of the dog. He couldn't possibly be alive now, after fifteen years, but I thought it polite to mention him. Her face tightened again.

"He turned savage. At least he bit Mr. Jenkins and had to be put to sleep." That prodded her memory in another direction and she asked had I a frock with long sleeves and not too short in the skirt. I told her I had not and she said, "Come with me."

Under the bed in my room was a cardboard box. Effie dragged it out and untied the several strings which held it. Its contents were mixed; a lot of photographs, most of them replicas of those I had seen at home; several strings of beads with other trinkets, a cookery book, a copy of *Gone with the Wind,* a hat that had been perky before it was squashed flat, some dainty underwear, and the dress Effie had worn on the day of the photograph. It was white, with little bunches of pink and blue flowers. This she lifted and shook out. That year even summer frocks had had sleeves to the elbow.

"On you," Effie said, with no great assurance, "they would be just long enough. And I will turn up the hem. . . . Jennie, I'm sorry about this, but he has his principles."

I said, truthfully, that what I wore didn't matter. "But it seems a shame to spoil your dress, Effie."

"It was doing no good hidden away. Nothing I had was suitable wear for an Elder's wife." Then she said a very significant thing. "On you the waist will be a bit low, but they are low this year." Something of the old Effie remained; she was still fashion conscious!

"What is Mr. Jenkins an Elder of?"

"The Chosen of Abraham."

"Is he a Jew?"

"Oh no, dear. He's Welsh. It's a sect, very small and special. But growing. We sometimes have as many as ten at a meeting nowadays."

"Are you one?"

"I try to be. I'm not a very good one, yet." She gave that little half-smile and I saw that her eyes were still very blue and pretty.

In the days that followed I realised that I had been very privileged to have been given, on arrival, a home-produced egg. I never had another. Mr. Jenkins' eggs were all large and brown and he had customers for them. Every morning, except Sunday, he loaded his estate car with eggs, with dressed fowls, with superb asparagus, new potatoes and peas, tomatoes and cucumbers and lettuces, and drove into Cheltenham where the three best hotels and greengrocers' shops absorbed them. On these journeys he did the necessary shopping. Effie never went with him—she was too busy.

To give Mr. Jenkins his due, he worked very hard, but Effie worked infinitely harder; for one thing, in addition to all she did out of doors, she cooked for us all and kept the house clean; for another all the heaviest work seemed to fall to her. She dug up the potatoes for example; she did a great deal of hoeing. Mr. Jenkins would kill a fowl and take it to the shed with its neck dangling; it was Effie who plucked it and got it ready for the oven.

So far as I could, I helped her and as we worked together we talked, with an especial liveliness when Mr. Jenkins was absent. As soon as his car was heard she'd go stiff and quiet. One hot morning he said he was having his hair cut; so he would be away longer and something like a holiday atmosphere made itself felt—though Effie did not cease to be busy. I—suitably clad as a member of an Elder's household—dashed down to the village shop and came back with a block of ice-cream, a packet of chocolate biscuits, and two bottles of chilled Coca-Cola. Effie's face lit up with guilty pleasure.

"I haven't had an ice-cream or a Coke since I left Cambridge," she said.

"Is it because of the money?" I asked. I could not help observing that we seldom ate the same thing. Mr. Jenkins had eggs and bacon for breakfast; Effie and I porridge; he had pork chop, we had stew—very good stew, Effie was a wonderful cook—but stew. He ate, with audible enjoyment, grilled sole, while Effie and I ate that nameless, very yellow fish that looks as though it were sold by the yard.

"No," Effie said, "I think he does very well." She added, loyally, "As he deserves to do. He works very hard."

"So do you. In fact I think you work harder than he does. So why shouldn't you have what you fancy?"

She said, "Jennie, you're too young to understand."

And that was the first time anyone had ever said that to me. I'd been too young to have a bicycle, too young, "a drag" on that picnic day; too young to go ski-ing; but never too young to understand. In our family understanding was taken for granted; a bit like fitting on shoes; all sizes were there, you took what fitted you best and left the rest, comfortably assured that one day you would understand more—fill a bigger shoe.

I said, "What don't I understand, Effie?"

"What being married means. Being one with another person."

I thought that over. The only married couple of whom I had really first-hand knowledge were my parents and no two people could be less alike—except where their work was concerned; but they were happy.

I said, draining the last of my Coke, "Are you *happy,* Effie?" She gave me a look. Then she said, "We all make our mistakes and we live with them. There he is now . . ." She picked up the two empty bottles, wrapped them in paper, and dropped them into the dustbin that stood outside the kitchen door.

I hated Mr. Jenkins.

With every bite or sup that he took, with every word he said, I hated him more and more. It seemed to me that he never opened his mouth except to feed it or to grumble. I never heard him say "thank you" to Effie or give a word of praise, but he was ready enough with a reprimand—"You left the hoe out," or "This is not to my liking," if his steak was not exactly right.

My stay under his roof was limited and never, never would I return. If anybody ever suggested it again I would say, "I'd sooner go to gaol." But I could not really look forward to my own liberation because I must leave Effie behind. And by this time she had inspired in me the same affection that had kept her name and her memory alive in our family all these years.

One day I said to her, "Effie, why don't you come back with me? You'd be very welcome."

"He would never agree."

"He needn't know. You could just come with me to the station and get on the train and never come back. You could live with us and be happy ever after."

"I'm married to him, Jennie. I stood there and of my own free will said for better or worse. I didn't know him then as I do now; but I said it and I must stick to it."

"People get divorced," I said.

"I know. But it is a confession of failure. And it is not as though . . . He is a hard-working, honest, God-fearing man."

"And selfish," I said. "And a bully."

She looked shocked; not angered. She seemed to have lost her capacity for anger, though the family legend credited her with quick temper and Margery said that she was the only person who had ever walloped her.

She now said, "Hush. You must not say such things. They aren't true. And you're under his roof."

"Your roof, too, Effie," I reminded her. I thought

how much I should have enjoyed my stay had it been solely her roof: even in his brief absences we worked up a kind of cheerfulness. "Why did you ever marry him?"

"You're too young to understand," she said again. She added, "I liked the idea of living in the country. I liked the thought of having some children of *my own*. . . . I made the mistake of thinking I was *good* enough. I've done my best to make up for that, though."

I said, almost gleefully—still being young enough to take pleasure in displaying my vocabulary, "Effie, you've got an inferiority complex. And *he* gave it to you! No wonder Whisky bit him! I'd bite him myself if I were a dog."

"You must not say such things. You do glare and scowl. And that only makes it worse for me."

That had an ominous ring. I asked, "Are you afraid of him?" I meant physically; anybody could see that she was afraid of displeasing him, anxious to avoid rebuke.

"Of course not," she said. "Why should I be?"

The dress that Effie had made for me began to grow grubby. It was ordinary cotton, not drip-dry; so to take its place while it was washed, dried, and ironed Effie proposed to turn two of my shameless shifts into one. They were both green, of differing shades, and Effie took pleasure in planning their union. Six inches off the skirt of the darker green, added to the skirt of the paler one, the bodice of the darker one made into decent elbow-length sleeves. "And if there's a scrap over, a narrow strip around the neck. It will be quite stylish."

I said I was sorry that she had all this to do on top of

everything else, but she said she liked sewing. I went to the village shop, but they had no green cotton. Effie said, "Never mind. I will ask Mr. Jenkins. At the right moment."

It came two mornings later when he said in his denunciatory way that one of the shops which bought stuff from him was closed for their *annual holiday*. He spoke these cheerful words as though naming some terrible vice. "So I will have to go to Gordon's."

Effie said, "That's next door to Bloom's. Would you just buy me two reels of green cotton?"

Even over so small a request, made at the right moment, he had to be awkward.

"There is always the traffic warden. Have you no other thread?"

"Only white and dark colours."

"Use what you have," he said.

I saw myself wearing a dress made out of two materials that differed in colour and texture and were sewn together with black or white thread. That did not dismay me much—though there were limits even to my clothes-carelessness: what angered me was that Effie's pleasure in her work was ruined. One of the family sayings was that whatever Effie took in hand she made a good job of. She wanted to make a good job of clothing me decently. . . . And then, in a flash I understood exactly what had happened to Effie. She had wanted to make a good job of being a wife, of being a Chosen of Abraham; just as she had wanted to make specially good pancakes, knit difficult Fair Isle sweaters, prop up our ramshackle household. Another popped into my mind—Effie was a perfectionist. It explained everything.

I offered to ride into Cheltenham with Mr. Jenkins and to buy the cotton while he delivered to Gordon's. This—I thought—sensible suggestion was slapped down. He had a very full load this morning and had no room for passengers. He spoke as though I were plural and all of us fat.

He then said that he would not come straight home; he had something to talk over with Mr. Blake.

The moment he had gone Effie said, "Off with that frock. I'll rub it through and have it ironed and back on you in a couple of hours. Mr. Blake is a great talker."

Coming down, wearing my shirt and jeans and carrying the frock, I said, "Effie, I'll wash it."

She said no; she'd wash it. If I wanted to do anything move the sprinkler. I did that and then ran down to the village shop. They were out of Coca-Cola so I bought a bottle of cider and some ice-cream.

Effie and I ate the ice-cream at once. While I was away she had washed the decent frock and cleaned out the place where the fowls slept, a revolting job for a hot morning; and hard, too, because chicken manure must not be put straight on to the earth which it is to enrich. It had to be put into a wheelbarrow and taken to a particular place to mature, mixed in with vegetable debris. Effie was glad of the ice-cream. Afterwards she dug the new potatoes for the next day's selling, made the fowl's mid-day meal—old potatoes, well mashed and mixed with meal—while I mounded up the celery bed. Nobody realised the labour that a sound white root of celery involved. It had to be shrouded in earth as it grew; exposed to the light the stuff would turn green;

mounded up, with only the leaves showing, it stayed white and was greatly in demand.

We were both hot, sweaty, and exhausted when, around eleven o'clock, we sat down to drink our cider which was cool because I had set it down under the sink.

I forget what we were talking about. I do know that it was not Mr. Jenkins, because as soon as I realised that it was something *in* Effie that had made her alter I had not mentioned him any more than I would mention cancer to somebody who had it. But we were talking about something and laughing and drinking our cider and suddenly *he* was there; in the open doorway.

She had denied that she was frightened of him; but it was fear that changed her colour and made the black of her eyes swamp the blue as she turned and saw him. She jumped up and stood with her back to the table, her arms slightly spread as though by taking up such a posture she could shield the cider, and me, improperly clad, from his sight. She said, "I did not expect you back so soon. But your dinner is well forward."

"So!" he said. "And now it is spiritous liquors. Under my very roof. I knew how it would be. For fifteen years I said no mention, no remembrance of that house of iniquity. Then they must gad off to the ends of the earth, with no care for their own and you say to me —She is only ten. You quote the Scriptures; suffer little children, you said." His voice was denunciatory, but cold and remote, like God rebuking somebody in the Old Testament. At the same time his sing-song way of speaking made it sound like poetry. "And I was fool enough to listen. So now there she sits, dressed as no girl-child should be; and you sit with her drinking *alcohol*."

I jumped up and stood beside Effie.

"It's my fault," I said. "I brought it in. I didn't know it was alcohol."

He reached out and took up the bottle and held it very close to my face.

"You can read, can you not? You that come of such a *clever* family."

The bottle was so close to me that I had to squint in order to read Maybower Cider's confession of alcoholic content. I remembered my father saying that he would sooner drink good English cider than Algerian plonk.

"Pour it down the sink," he said. I did so, greatly surprised to find that my hands were shaking. Why? I certainly was not scared of him. "And the glasses," he said. I emptied away the pitiable remains. I felt that he watched me with pleasure and I thought of another new word I had learned lately—sadist.

"Now," he said, "begin to get your gear together. You go on the first train tomorrow."

Nothing could have suited me better, except that it meant leaving Effie behind, alone with this dreadful man.

I said, "Please, Mr. Jenkins, don't be cross with Ef . . . with Mrs. Jenkins. It was entirely my fault."

"She has offended God," he said.

I went upstairs and began to pack. Some of what was said in the kitchen was audible. Effie—and I thought it was very brave of her—tried to plead for me. "She is only ten." "An empty house." "Only another week anyway." His voice carried better: he said that young as I was I had led her astray because she was willing to be corrupted. She had a will like water and backward-looking eye. He said evil was like the leprosy. And he was adamant about my leaving on the morrow.

And all because we had drunk not quite a full glass of cider apiece!

I packed the two green frocks which now would never be made one. I looked out of the window and saw the flowered one which I should never wear again, hanging on the line. I saw the garden, neat as a piece of embroidery, and the two greenhouses; one full of ripening tomatoes, the other of pot-plants, primulas, cynararias, cyclamen, and chrysanthemums being brought on for early marketing in the autumn. They would all be sold, to cheer other homes, I thought. Effie would no more have a flowering plant than she had had asparagus and strawberries.

She called up the stairs, "Dinner is ready, Jennie." I knew by her voice that she had been crying. Over my indecent jeans and shirt I put on the dressing-gown which, handed down from Angela, was full long. Mr. Jenkins ate braised oxtail with good appetite; I ate stew; Effie pretended to. We did not speak a word.

One of the little jobs which I had voluntarily assumed was the watering of the plants in the greenhouse as soon as the sun moved away from it in the afternoon. In June, when I arrived this had been between five and six o'clock; now it was earlier; the first week in August, the turn of the year. Soon after four o'clock.

Mr. Jenkins had spent the afternoon tying his runner beans on to their iron-framework; Effie dressed three fowls and again mounded up the celery. I had not been idle and when, at five o'clock, we were together in

the kitchen, drinking the tea—made to Mr. Jenkins'
taste and very black—Effie had once said to me that at
first she had disliked it, but you could get used to anything. I said,

"While I was watering I saw some greenfly on the
plants."

Those who bring bad news are never popular; and
I was in disgrace anyway. He gave me a very unfriendly look indeed.

"Only on Thursday I fumigated," he said. He spoke
as though I were to blame; and he was right. Greenfly
are quite easily transferred. He then turned his attention to Effie.

"I was about to get The Room ready," he said. I
broke into a light sweat. This was Tuesday, when the
Chosen of Abraham had an evening gathering. I
thought, for a moment, that he was going to tell Effie
to fumigate. But he did not. He took a key from a hook
on the dresser and handed it to her.

"You go," he said. "Open the windows first and do
not forget to dust the rungs of the chairs. I will be
along." The Room was the Holy of Holies to the
Chosen of Abraham and ordinarily Mr. Jenkins main-
tained it. Perhaps in the past he had entrusted the
task to Effie and she had overlooked the rungs of the
chairs. Effie crammed on the hideous hat which made
her look like something out of the ark, but without
which it was indecent for the wife of an Elder to walk a
quarter of a mile through a village street, and hurried
away. Mr. Jenkins went to the cupboard and took a
box of matches, and set off for the shed where he kept
tools, pesticides and fertilisers, stakes, flowerpots, and
such things.

I waited for a minute; then I went to the celery rows. I had worked on them in the morning, Effie had worked on them in the afternoon, but there was still a lot to be done. I did not do much. I got myself into position and watched. The door of the greenhouse was open. He went in, carrying the bowl of what looked like coarse dark tobacco shreds. He closed the door by giving it a push with his elbow. He shut the ventilator in the roof. Then he emptied the shreds on to the floor and struck a match. Smoke rose thin and blue at first, then thicker and greyer. I lost sight of him until he came to the door. There happened to him what had once happened to me, in a house we had hired at the seaside. It fronted on to the beach, so even a five-year-old could go in and out freely. I went in, to the bathroom, and when I was ready to come out the doorknob came off in my hand and when I tried to fit in on again the bar thing that connects the knobs and works the catch ran away from me. I was there for three hours. I now saw Mr. Jenkins try to fit this knob on again. I heard the outer knob and the connection fall on to the concrete outside.

I could hardly breathe, the suspense was so great. A sensible person would at this point have smashed a pane in the upper half of the door and stuck his head out to escape the fumes which were, Effie had said, when first we watched this operation together, very deadly and it did make you wonder about cigarettes, didn't it? But Mr. Jenkins, as his treatment of Effie proved, was not a sensible man. Or possibly he remembered that a pane of glass now cost a pound to replace.

He vanished into the smoke, now very thick, and I guessed he had thought of the ventilator. It worked on a kind of ratchet, rather like a saw, and it now lacked a few vital teeth. It could close all right, it would not open.

I like to think that he could *still* have smashed a pane. He had a chance—like in Russian Roulette. In fact I waited, agonised, for the sound of breaking glass. It did not come.

The Bird Bath

Opening her door for the first time to Mr. Mitson, Mrs. Pryor felt a sense of recoil. He looked like a tramp of the kind not often seen nowadays. He had a very red face, sharp red-rimmed little eyes, and a week's growth of beard. He wore a dirty old army greatcoat, made for a bigger man, and a hat which had long ago lost its original colour and shape. He smelled strongly of beer.

Nearby, however, actually in her tiny drive, stood a reassuring sight, a white pony, plump and shiny and with the placid look of a well-treated animal. Attached to the pony was a small cart, bearing in white paint the words—J. Mitson, Dealer. This morning J. Mitson was dealing in firewood.

He touched his hat civilly and said, "Morning, lady; I seen you just moved in and I happened on this—" He indicated the wood. "Just right, I said to myself, for the new lady. Dirt cheap, too. Three bob a basket or fifteen bob the lot."

She made her first mistake then by failing to inquire how many basketfuls the cart contained and by not keeping an eye on him as he unloaded. Mr. Mitson was always careful not to underatke any exertion likely to cause strain, and he went from cart to shed several times with the basket half full. Mrs. Pryor found an apple for the pony, and when Mr. Mitson rattled away with rather more than fifty per cent profit, he was satisfied that he had found a soft touch.

Not the man to neglect an opportunity, he sold her, in quick order, a sack of mixed bulbs—"Bit late for planting," he agreed, "but they'll come up, given time"; a length of chestnut fencing which he reckoned would just fit the gap in her hedge, and it did, as though it had been measured; a bundle of rose bushes—"None the worse for being without labels. All scented, which I know ladies like"; and a copper cauldron—"Minute I seen it I thought of you, lady. Polished up a bit, coupla plants in it. Look lovely in your hall."

He was persuasive, but never wheedling; all his arguments had a backing of good sense; his approach was jaunty, take it or leave it, I'm doing *you* a favour. But there was a kind of inevitability about him; she felt that one day, sooner or later, he would talk her into buying something that she didn't need, something she couldn't afford or positively disliked.

She felt that this day had arrived when he arrived with a load of turf, done up in outsize Swiss rolls. The people from whom she had bought the little house had had five children, and all that remained of the lawn were a few dispirited tufts of coarse grass. "I knew you was the sort of lady that'd want a lawn," Mr. Mitson said. "So the moment I seen this, I said to myself, that'll do her nicely."

"Well, I don't know," Mrs. Pryor said doubtfully. "I *had* rather thought of having the lawn levelled and seeded."

"Be a coupla years before you had a lawn worth looking at. And grass seed is very expensive."

The white pony, who also knew a soft touch when it met one, gently jingled its bridle. Mrs. Pryor fetched and presented the offering. "It's a question of *laying* it, Mr. Mitson," she said. "I don't think I could manage it."

Mr. Mitson stroked his chin with its week's growth of beard that never varied. "I see," he said. "Well, look here. I might, I don't know, but I might find somebody who'd do it for you. If I can it's a deal, if not I'll take it along to the cimiterry, they're always on the lookout for good turf." In a short time he was back with two men, one old, one very young, who were prepared to lay her lawn. To them she happened to say that she wished the lawn to end about six feet from the back of the house as she hoped, one day, to have a tiny paved terrace. Halfway through the following week Mr. Mitson arrived with a load of broken paving stones. The same two men came and made her little terrace.

On the whole, she reflected, as she looked around, Mr. Mitson had served her well. She had a supply of firewood, the fencing, a lawn, an area of paving; and in her hall the copper pot, though larger than the space warranted, glowed brightly and looked well. Out of sight the bulbs and the rose bushes were, she hoped, getting ready to flower. So why, she wondered, should she always feel a slight apprehension and ask herself, "What now?" when she heard the white pony's hoofs?

She did not hear them in the first ten days of January. Those who knew Mr. Mitson's habits could have told her that he ceased general dealing and most other activities when the thermometer fell below 37 degrees F. When, with the onset of a warmer spell, she heard him, she braced herself to tell him that she now had everything she needed and must spend nothing at all for quite a time.

She could not even guess at what lay, all alone on the cart's floor, shrouded in sackcloth; it was not very large, but she judged it to be heavy since Mr. Mitson invited her to step out and take a look, rather than bringing it to the door. "It's a beauty," he said. "Ever since you put down that bit of paving, I been on the lookout for you." He whisked off the sacking and revealed a stone column about eighteen inches square and three feet long. It lay on its side. It was rather mossy; it was carved. She was rather relieved to see its apparent uselessness; it enabled her to say quite firmly, "It is interesting, Mr. Mitson, but I don't want it. It would be of no earthly use to me."

He was taken aback at this, her first piece of sales resistance. "What? No use? I thought all ladies liked a nice little bird bath."

Mrs. Pryor said, "Oh! A bird bath?"

"What did you reckon? I don't know about you, but

I think that'd look just the job on your bit of paving. Uncommon, too."

She had now had time to see that where the column ended in a solid plinth there was a worn hollow, about eight inches across and four deep. The thing had not, she felt almost certain, been intended to benefit birds, but it would make an admirable and most unusual bird bath.

"You go and try to buy one," Mr. Mitson said. "Charge you the earth, and just concrete. This is stone. And only three pound ten."

"I will have it," she said. "And then, Mr. Mitson, I really must stop buying things, however nice or cheap. I intended to spread the expense of making the garden over a year."

"You'd have spent a lot more in the end." He stepped out into the road and, placing two fingers in his mouth, blew a piercing whistle. The younger of the two men who had laid the turf and the paving hurried out from his lurking place and with some purely symbolic assistance from Mr. Mitson, brought the bird bath and set it down upon the spot indicated by Mrs. Pryor, on the little paved space opposite the french window of her sitting-room.

"Settled down a treat," Mr. Mitson said, taking the money.

By this time Mrs. Pryor had discovered that, though milder than recent days, this was not really a warm morning and that she had been unwise to leave the house without a coat. She was shivering quite violently. She also had a feeling of anxiety, concerned with being alone, with a bad chill, or even influenza. She had as yet made no contact in the small town, except with

those who supplied her needs—and Mr. Mitson; she
had indeed only one real friend in the whole of England. She had herself been born and had spent much
of her life in Africa and had chosen this area because
Simon, her late husband, had remembered it with
sentimental affection, having spent holidays there with
an aunt, long since dead. Widowed, she had come to
England, hoped to find a cheap house in Simon's be-
loved East Anglia, and had done so. Until this moment
she had not been conscious of loneliness—except in
the sense that without Simon she would always be
lonely. Now, shivering, and feeling vaguely ill, she
realised the state of her isolation. She did not even
know the name of a doctor. She thought, with a terrible
pang, *I could be ill, I could die and nobody would
notice, except the milkman!*

However, once indoors again, and fortified by a cup
of tea, the feeling of malaise and of fear wore off. It
was simply the cold, to which she was unaccustomed;
one must not get into a panic over nothing. She had
lived through far more perilous situations than being
alone and threatened by a chill, in a small English town.

As she drank her tea she looked out of the window
and took pleasure in the sight of the bird bath, standing
sturdily outside the window. It was exactly right, both
ornamental and useful. Restored, she took a jug of
water and some broken crusts, and putting on a coat,
went out to minister to the birds. She poured the water
into the hollow, shared the crusts round its rim, and
almost immediately was again aware that she felt ill
and was absolutely alone. In her mind a curious phrase
took shape: *Sick unto death and abandoned by all.*

She had decided against having a telephone for the

time being. In her friendless state, it seemed an un-
warranted extravagance. If, as she hoped, she made
friends, and if, again as she hoped, she found some job
within her rather limited capacity, that would be time
enough to think about installing a telephone. Now she
saw it, not as a luxury, but as an absolute necessity.
She went indoors and wrote the letter of application,
and on her way to post it she stopped at a little general
shop and asked the woman who usually served her to
tell her the name and address of a doctor.

The woman provided the information and said,
"Feeling poorly?" Mrs. Pryor was so overcome by
even this small amount of personal interest that she
almost broke into tears. Before she could reply the
woman said, "There's a lot of 'flu about," and she
seemed to draw away a little as though anxious not to
be infected.

Towards the end of her stay in Africa Mrs. Pryor
had become accustomed to slights, both open and
covert, but nothing had hurt so deeply as this hardly
perceptible recoil. Such easily wounded susceptibility
she took to be another symptom of an impending cold.
She went home, made up the fire and drew the curtains
and decided that the best thing she could do to take her
mind off her misery was to write a few letters. A
married couple, close friends who had lately been in
the same situation as herself, had opted for South
Africa, thinking the English climate too severe. She
wrote to them, faintly astonished to find that she was
writing gaily, about how cosy her tiny house was, about
the compensations of the English winter, about the
bulbs and rose trees she had planted and how much
she looked forward to the spring. She wrote in the

same vein to two other friends who, having little choice, had decided to "stick it out" in Tsalasi.

And she wrote to her one friend in England, hard-headed, foresighted Ethel Bradford who years ago had gone to Oxford, taken her degree, got a job as a teacher, and never looked back. She found that with Ethel her tone changed slightly. Moods were a bit like hats: you wore one for this occasion, another for another, and she had no need to pretend to Ethel who had said, when they met in London, "You'll be very lonely, Kathy." To Ethel she could admit that she was lonely. And yet the other letters were not false, or intended to convey the wrong impression. It was just—she halted her pen and worked the thought out—the friends who had stayed in Tsalasi and the friends who had gone to South Africa had enough troubles of their own; they needed cheerful letters. Ethel's response to her admission of loneliness would be a healthy, if faintly smug reflection—I was right!

Her feeling of isolation and impending illness waned as she wrote, but as a precaution she took aspirin and a hot blackcurrant drink upon retiring. When she woke, she felt perfectly well.

Ethel's response to her letter was unexpected; a telegram. "If agreeable propose visit, Friday to Monday. Arrive 11.30 a.m."

The idea of having company for a long week-end was exhilarating in the extreme; she laid in a modest stock of special fare and bought a second hot-water bottle. From time to time she felt unwell, but the expected cold never developed and she hoped that it would not do so during the visit and thus ruin it.

Ethel brought her brisk, kindly, slightly astringent

headmistress's manner with her. "Nobody is likely to knock on your door, Kathy, and ask if you are lonely. You *must join* something: the Townswomen's Guild; the Business and Professional Women's Club—they accept housewives nowadays. In a town even as small as this, there must be some cultural activities: an art society or something to do with music." Ethel would have been a member of five groups within a month—and President within a year.

"I know," Mrs. Pryor said meekly. "I thought I'd leave it until I was settled in." She was of a very retiring disposition and rather dreaded the business. Also she was not quite certain how one set about joining things.

"The local librarian is in a position to be helpful," Ethel said. "Librarians are mines of information."

After an interval Ethel tackled the problem of finding some useful and remunerative employment for her friend. "I've given this matter some thought," she said. "You're absolutely unqualified, that's the trouble; but that is easily remedied nowadays. Naturally, I thought of teaching, an understaffed profession; and I'm practically certain you'd find something if you wrote to the Director of Education and said you were willing to take an unqualified post—for you I thought Domestic Science—and would take a crash course in the holidays."

"Am I not a little old to start training?"

"Good gracious no. At a College of Further Education in which I am interested, fifty per cent of the students are over thirty." Mrs. Pryor's plans for finding some job to eke out her very limited means had been much more humble, much less brisk. But she did not say so.

By this time they had finished tea. Mrs. Pryor refused help in the washing of cups, "No, no, Ethel, this is your holiday." Ethel sat down to complete *The Times* crossword puzzle.

The kitchen window also overlooked the paved area, and the light from it, mingling with the last daylight, revealed to Mrs. Pryor one last, late roosting bird on the bird bath. The scraps she had put out after lunch had vanished immediately, and the water bowl was empty again because birds were feckless; they bathed, no matter how cold the air; they splashed; they wasted. She felt sorry for this lone latecomer, so she filled a jug and took up the crusts she had cut from the tea-time sandwiches.

Standing by the bird bath, she knew that her fear had become reality; the illness that had threatened struck suddenly. A fit of shivering, the worst she had yet known, came upon her, rattling her teeth. She was so weak and dizzy that to prevent herself from falling she had to clutch at the solid stone; and clinging, sagging, she felt, despite Ethel's proximity, utterly alone. *Sick unto death and abandoned by all.* Ethel, she knew, would desert her; recoil as the woman in the shop had done, at the least hint of infection. Ethel had, on the Tuesday, a very important conference to attend; Ethel could not afford to take chances with her health. And why should she?

Nevertheless, feeling her fingers weaken, knowing that she was about to fall, she cried, "Ethel. Help me!"

Inside the sitting-room, the curtains slid back; the french window opened and Ethel came out hastily.

"Kathy! What is . . . ?" Strong arms held her, heaved her, brought her into the sitting-room, put her in a chair, and pushed her head down on to her knees. Ethel's reliable, unruffled voice said, "You're all right. Concentrate on taking some deep breaths. There. Better now?"

"Better," Mrs. Pryor said, raising her head. "That is . . . the puzzling thing. That was the worst yet, but I've had little spells before. I just feel terribly ill, deserted by God and man . . . and then I'm all right."

"Have you consulted a doctor?" Ethel asked.

"No. It has only happened lately. I just feel as ill as possible for a second or two, and then, to be honest, I quite forget about it."

"You must see a doctor tomorrow."

He was a young man with a hurried manner, but he took his time over her, giving her much the same examination as he would have done had he been examining her for an insurance company. Heart, lungs, blood-pressure, reflexes. He said that, so far as he could tell by such a cursory examination, she seemed in good health. He said that if the attacks continued, they must go into the matter more thoroughly.

They went to have coffee at a café which Mrs. Pryor had visited once and could assure Ethel was a "nice" place. There was a vacant table for which Mrs. Pryor would have made, but Ethel said, "Wait!" She ran an unerring eye over the occupied tables—those that were set for four and occupied by two; chose her quarry and moved in. Within two minutes conversation was general and animated. Presently she mentioned her own name, adding that she was just a visitor; she mentioned Mrs. Pryor's name—"She has come to live here because of a family tie." This led to explanations and one of the women said, "I never knew Miss Pryor, but my mother was very fond of her. In fact she left my mother a worktable and a set of prints. I have them now. You must come and see them, Mrs. Pryor."

"You see," Ethel said afterwards, meaningfully. "You would have gone to the empty table and spoken to no-one. Now you have an invitation to tea next Thursday. And that should lead on."

"You're wonderful, Ethel, I always thought so . . ." It was true; she had always admired Ethel, who had been outstanding even in school; perfect, then Head Girl.

They drifted into reminiscent talk about the school-days they had shared; brushing away the faint nostalgia, laughing almost girlishly over remembered pranks, the eccentricities of those who had taught them. Ethel helped with the clearing up after lunch; and she carried the meal's debris out to the object which was both bird bath and bird table.

Coming back with the emptied plate in her hand she said, "You know, Kathy, a thought just struck me. We laugh, even now, about Miss Patterson's hair coming down in that hockey match. I suppose some of my girls find me equally comic and a quarter of a century from now . . . Really, what a sobering thought."

Mrs. Pryor said, "Ethel, what a thought for *you* of all people! Miss Patterson, with her hair up or down, *was* comic. Claiming descent from King Arthur and all that nonsense."

On this afternoon, Ethel volunteered to make tea. "I've never had time to become fully domesticated,"

she said, "but at least I can make a cup of tea." She
looked at Mrs. Pryor who was mixing the stuffing for
the next day's roast chicken, and said, "You should
have a kitchen stool, you know. Many jobs can be
done just as well sitting down."

"Oh, I'm all right," Mrs. Pryor said, mixing
vigorously. "As a matter of fact, so far as I can
remember, I've never had a silly turn because of any
exertion."

A chance not to be missed by Miss Bradford. She
said, "Kathy, you know, I have been wondering, and
what you have just said confirms my thought. It may be
psychosomatic. Being alone, not having enough to
occupy you . . ."

"That tea-cake is blazing," Mrs. Pryor said. They
had bought tea-cakes at the "nice" place.

Extinguishing the flame, Miss Bradford said, "That
shows what comes of trying to do two things at once."
She added, "I'm sorry, Kathy. I'm afraid it's ruined."

"It will do for the birds," Mrs. Pryor said. Following
her habit of never deferring to the next moment the
thing to be done in this, Miss Bradford crumbled the
ruined tea-cake and took it out. She did not return
immediately; the kettle boiled, Mrs. Pryor abandoned
the stuffing and made the tea. It took only a second or
two, but in carrying the pot to the kettle she came
level with the window and saw Ethel standing by the
bird bath, halted in the gesture of brushing black
crumbs from her fingers. And it struck her suddenly
that Ethel looked *old*. That had not been her impression
when they met in London; or yesterday. But now, well,
there it was, Ethel looked old, far older than her age
which was a year and a half more than Mrs. Pryor's.

And the strange thing was that, coming back into the kitchen, Ethel having said, "So after all you had to make the tea. Dear me, I seem not to have made a very good job of it . . ." she also said, "Kathy, I was just looking round and thinking that when the time comes for me to retire, I should like a little place like this. Nobody can work for ever . . . I seldom look ahead in that particular way, but the thought did strike me. Try as one may to keep up with new ideas, there is a limit. Even the most successful career must end." She spoke rather like a child suddenly confronted with the fact that two and two made four.

"Life itself must end," said Mrs. Pryor, who had faced this fact with a somewhat similar surprise when her husband died.

Ethel said, "That is true." Then added, "That is a morbid way of thinking. If one thought about the final end of all human effort, no effort would be made; and then where should we be?"

They drank their tea; ate the unburned tea-cakes and were soon deeply engaged with the puzzles, the testing of wits, of general knowledge which a thoughtfully considerate paper had provided for readers in need of some diverson over the week-end.

Next day the birds in Mrs. Pryor's garden ate well and washed vigorously in the bowl, three times replenished. Once, scraping the rather sticky remains of the chocolate pudding on the flat surface that ringed the bowl, Mrs. Pryor again felt unwell, but this time, instead of remaining out in the cold and clutching at the chilly stone, she staggered back into the kitchen and leaned on the draining board until she recovered, which she soon did. She said nothing to Ethel, for she had already conducted some searching inquiries as to what Kathy ate when she was alone. The mysterious spells, if not entirely imaginary, might be due to lack of calories or vitamins. Mrs. Pryor loved and deeply admired Ethel, but she could at times be rather overwhelming.

Monday was clear and bright, though cool. Mrs. Pryor was busy converting what remained of the chicken into a toothsome dish, but Ethel was at a loss what to do. Presently she said, "From what I can see of that bird bath, Kathy, it is rather finely carved. Would you mind if I removed the moss and took a closer look?"

"I should be glad. I've been meaning to do it myself."

She gave Ethel a short, sturdy vegetable knife, pointed in a way that facilitated the removal of eyes from potatoes. Now and again, as she made the pastry and the sauce for the chicken vol-au-vents, she glanced out to see how Ethel was getting on. As usual, well. The green moss fell away like the rind of a fruit; the point of the knife, pecking away, cleared the soil-filled interstices; moment by moment more of the carving became visible.

Mrs. Pryor turned away and stooped to light her oven. When next she looked out from the kitchen window, Ethel, the job finished, had gone. Upstairs, Mrs. Pryor imagined, to wash her hands. The oven heated; Mrs. Pryor placed the vol-au-vent cases in the correct position and adjusted the regulator. Then she went to the bottom of the stairs and called, "Ethel! Sherry time!" There was no answer; in fact the silence hung heavy almost as though she were alone in the house.

Then, close behind her the front door opened, letting in a flow of cold air, and slammed. And there was Ethel. "I just ran out to make a telephone call," she said. "I changed my mind about something rather important."

"Come and have some sherry," Mrs. Pryor said.

They were both just old enough to adhere to the now discredited custom of saying something, even if it were only *"Cheerio"* before drinking. Ethel said, "Happy days, Kathy," and Mrs. Pryor said, "Happy days, Ethel; and a nice conference."

"I'm not going. That was why I had to telephone in such a hurry. I had to let Mr. Feilding know." She drank her sherry and allowed her glass to be refilled. Then she said, "Kathy, do you know what your bird bath *is?*"

"You mean what it was originally? No. I somehow never thought that it was intended for birds. What is it, Ethel?"

"I can't be sure, of course, not being an expert; but I should say that it was the lower half of a marker or boundary cross. The carving is definitely of a religious nature. Such crosses were common at one time; some vanished at the Reformation, others in Cromwellian times. The crosses were relatively fragile, the plinths heavy, so they were left in place and even served a certain purpose. Either as a place where charitably minded people could leave food for lepers . . ."

"Oh no!" Mrs. Pryor exclaimed in the way people do when accepting a horrid truth.

"I'm sorry, Kathy," Ethel said, remembering after all these years how Kathy could never bear the sight of a bruise or a hacked shin after a hockey game. "But, you must admit, it is interesting, and most unusual, to find such a relic in a private garden."

Sick unto death and abandoned by all. Mrs. Pryor remembered the odd phrase; and the feeling of being ill all over; of facing death in complete isolation. She had felt it first by the bird bath; and now that she came to think about it, each subsequent time; there, and there only. She had known, just for a few seconds, through something more subtle than imagination, what it meant to be stricken, doomed, and outcast. The misery had impregnated the stone and the stone had given it back.

She sat, silent and stunned, concentrating upon preserving her composure lest Ethel should guess. Ethel would think she was mad!

Ethel said, nodding toward the bird bath where a blackbird was wasting water, "Doing that little job cleared my mind. The carving, you really must look at it, Kathy, is so exquisite, so detailed. On the farther side, the feeding of the five thousand, and you can see the scales on the fish. I scratched away and I thought, All that dedicated work; and to end as a bird bath! I saw the analogy. I have always done the donkey work for the E.P.M.S. and Mr. Feilding has always taken all the credit. He sounded quite shattered just now when I told him I did not mean to attend." She lifted her glass and drank the sherry as though it were the blood of an enemy.

Mrs. Pryor thought, with horror, Yes, with me physical weakness and feeling lonely, my vulnerable points; with her, a different approach. A leaching away of confidence and ambition. Because some of those who came in the night, walking on maimed feet, groping with maimed hands . . . ambitious once, careers cut suddenly short . . .

She said, completely reversing their roles, "Ethel, I think you were hasty. I'm afraid you will regret such an impulsive action. I know, from your letters what . . ." she would have liked to give the organisation its full, pompous name, but she could only remember Educational Projects . . . "what E.P.M.S. means to you. I'm so afraid that just because you removed that moss . . ." She checked herself.

"Really, Kathy," Miss Bradford said, "the moss had nothing to do with it. The carving, yes, that had a catalytic effect. Up to a point. But I was not hasty or impulsive. I had been meditating drastic action for a long time. Mr. Feilding knows what to do if he wishes assistance from me in future."

Mr. Feilding knew, and he acted. The telegram arrived soon after lunch. "Exactly what I expected," Ethel said, looking pleased.

"You will be going, after all?"

"Yes. And I shall take the chair. Mr. Feilding has developed a sudden cold. In his feet," Ethel said incisively.

She spent the rest of her visit exhorting Kathy; a sermon with many headings. She was to eat at least one full meal a day; return to the doctor if the little turns persisted; make the most of her invitation to tea, cultivating the friendship of her hostess and anyone else who might be there; she was to get in touch with the Education Committee.

To this Mrs. Pryor added another thing to be done; she must get Mr. Mitson to remove that haunted stone.

She would pay him to whistle up his accomplice and take it away.

Well into February she waited, eager now to hear the rattle of the white pony's hoofs. It did not come. Mr. Mitson had done a little general dealing in copper wire, the property of the Electricity Board, and in view of his many previous convictions the magistrates had, as they said, no alternative.

What scraps she now had to offer the birds Mrs. Pryor placed on the kitchen windowsill; rain, and sometimes snow, replenished the little hollow. Very gradually, but with patient persistence, the moss re-formed over the carvings.

Something Young About the House

While she had lived alone Kathy Allbright had adopted a haphazard attitude towards food, but now that Maria was with her she served two solid meals every day: breakfast promptly at five minutes to eight, so that Maria could catch the bus at half past, and supper at seven. Her midday meal Maria took at school with the boarders. Kathy had never visited Germany, and knew nothing of German cookery, but she had asked Maria what she *liked* to eat. Maria had taken the opportunity to show once again that she liked nothing and nobody, and Kathy had thought, *She's terribly homesick, poor child.* And she had gone on making efforts to please, to alleviate, to cheer.

The girl had now been in England for three weeks, and at school for two, and across the supper table Kathy asked with forced brightness, "Well, Maria, do you like school any better after a fortnight?"

"I am hating it."

For the first time Kathy allowed herself to wonder whether the girl was hostile as well as homesick. Such short, brusque answers, such unresponsive glances! Wouldn't a genuinely homesick fifteen-year-old in an alien land tend to appreciate kindness?

I must not think that way—not of Constance's child, Kathy told herself. She made another effort. "Has Rosemary looked after you?"

Rosemary, the daughter of Kathy's doctor, was also a day girl at the school. Kathy had asked her, privately, to do what she could to make Maria's entry into school as pleasant as possible. With a rather touching solemnity, Rosemary had promised to do so.

"She is telling me what to do and where to go." Maria spoke as though she were a prisoner. Then she said, "I am too old to be a schoolgirl."

"Oh, no. Girls stay at school until they are eighteen."

"It is right for them. In their minds they are young." For the first time since her arrival she showed some spark of animation, some desire to communicate. "Today—it is Friday, fish pie and apple pudding. As we eat, of what, do you think, they talk? Ghost stories. You know what I mean? Tales of haunting."

"I should have thought that was interesting," said Kathy, who had a half-fearful weakness for such tales.

"Why interesting? In kindergarten, perhaps. But these are my-age girls. To be telling fairy tales!"

"There is a difference between ghosts and fairies," Kathy said. She couldn't really imagine Rosemary and the rest of swapping fairy tales over the fish pie.

"It is the same. They do not exist. Fairies and ghosts and werewolves and *Doppelgängers*. All the same. Nonsense."

Kathy reflected that Maria's father, a mining engineer probably had reared his daughter to scepticism. Yet something made her wish to defend the schoolgirls.

"Ghosts may be nonsense to you, but there are people, some quite clever people, who believe in ghosts."

"And you are one of those?"

"I don't know. I should say that I have an open mind."

"An open mind. That is idiom I must remember."

Maria applied herself to stewed plums and custard in a way that showed that for her the subject was closed.

Presently Kathy tried again. "Tomorrow," she said, "I have some work to deliver in Avonford; then, if it is a nice day, we could go on to Lambsmere and get a breath of sea air."

"Would it be possible to swim?"

"If it is as warm as today. Would you like to ask Rosemary if she is free to come with us?"

"It is for you to say."

Maria's voice expressed profound indifference, and Kathy heard, with dismay, a touch of sharpness in her own voice as she said, "I asked *you,* Maria. It makes no difference to me. I simply thought that it might be nicer for you to have someone of your own age."

"Then it is no, I do not wish to ask her. I am having enough of girls in the week." She rose, and it was plain that it would be left this evening, as on former ones, for Kathy to wash the dishes. "I am now writing to my father."

For the first time Kathy corrected Maria's English.

"You are now going to write to your father," she said. "If you say, 'I am now writing,' it means you are doing it now."

"Thank you," Maria said, without gratitude.

"Try to write him a cheerful letter," Kathy said. "After all, he's far from home too; and it isn't much fun for him to hear how miserable you are."

"He is to blame for my misery; he could have taken me with him."

"You know that isn't true. In that region of Brazil there is no accommodation for females. He wanted you to go to an English school, and I think that was very sensible of him. After all, you are half English."

That remark Maria ignored, in a disconcerting way she had, and went off to the spare room which Kathy had fitted out as a bedroom-study.

Kathy thought of the usual excuses: the girl was homesick, and undomesticated because she had spent so much time in places where labour was cheap and plentiful. Tonight, however, the excuses flowed less generously than usual. She faced for the first time the possibility that Maria disliked her. What had she done wrong? Childless herself and leading a rather lonely life, she had looked forward to welcoming the daughter of her favourite cousin and of Willi von Lodau, a man of such charm that even the elder members of the family, disapproving of the match—it was soon after the war—had quickly forgiven him for being a German. She had met Maria at the airport and been delighted to see how much she looked like her dead mother. Maria's first words had been, "My father says I am to call you Aunt Kathy." In the ensuing three weeks she had never again used the term.

It is possible, Kathy thought, *that she holds me to blame for her being here;* but the alternative was boarding school, as Willi had made plain. It was also possible that something in her greeting had offended teen-age dignity; perhaps she should not have thrown her arms around the girl and kissed her and said how much she had been looking forward . . .

Whatever the reason, the truth was that now, after three weeks, they were on no better terms. *And*—she thought—*I've taken on a lot of extra work and cooking, and all for what?* Then she was ashamed. It was too soon to judge; the child had been uprooted, she was disappointed at not being taken to Brazil, school was strange, England a foreign land. *I must be patient,* Kathy told herself, as she put the last plate away and scuttled off to the little room where she did the typing and duplicating by which she had eked out her income since she had been widowed, eight years ago.

Saturday was another Indian-summer day, warm and mild. Having delivered the finished work—two thousand copies of a circular letter appealing for funds to restore the little Georgian theatre—Kathy drove Maria to Lambsmere. And there, in the cold but placid sea, Maria bathed, and emerged as changed as the cripples of Biblical times who entered the pool at Bethesda. She'd been just as homesick, or hostile, just as sullen, throughout the drive; finally Kathy had given up trying to talk. The outing, the picnic meal, were wasted; and this could go on for a year, Kathy thought, and she must bear it.

Then Maria, smiling, had come out of the sea, said she was hungry, said what a lovely place this was, what a lovely picnic. And she said "Aunt Kathy" again and again. It was all suddenly exactly as Kathy had imagined it when she had written to Willi von Lodau and said that there was no need for inquiries about boarding schools, that Maria could live with her and attend Ashley House, that she herself was lonely and would love to have Maria's company. She had written, "It will be so nice for me to have somebody young about the house." She reproached herself for being impatient, a too-quick despairer, overcritical, lacking in understanding. All the way back, under the chatter and the laughter, she rebuked and admonished herself. Greedy, grasping, touchy!

They had left home before the milkman called, and, as was her habit on such occasions, Kathy had left on the windowsill of the kitchen two small plastic indicators. The blue one, set at figure "3," was for milk; the white one, set at "1," had mutely requested one carton of cream. But on this evening, having put the car in the garage, she saw, ranged along the windowsill, six bottles of milk, six cartons of cream.

"The milkman must have gone mad!" Kathy exclaimed; but a glance at the indicators showed her that both had been turned as far as they would go, to "6." Somebody's idea of a joke?

She had no time to ponder the mystery, for inside the house the telephone began to ring, and she hastened to answer it, carrying with her Maria's comforting words. "I will put them in the refrigerator, Aunt Kathy."

And when the telephone conversation—an unpleasant complaint from the customer to whom she had delivered work that morning—was concluded, it was a consolation to find that Maria had set the table, and begun to heat the soup. After supper Maria helped to clear the table; and she wiped the dishes. Evidently the homesickness had vanished, and with it the sullenness that Kathy, now self-reproachfully, held that she had imagined.

On Thursdays it had long been her habit to drive into Avonford and play bridge with her friend Alice Coffie, her mother who was crippled by arthritis, and a woman named Lucy Binder who lived in one of the flats over Alice's dress shop. On the Thursday after Maria's arrival Kathy had excused herself, saying she did not like to leave the girl alone during her first week. Sometime during the following week she had mentioned her regular outing, and suggested that Maria should ask Rosemary Broome to spend the evening with her, or that she should spend the evening at the Broomes'. Maria had been scornful of both ideas. She was accustomed, she said, to being left alone.

On this Thursday, however, as soon as Kathy began preparations for leaving the house, Maria said, "May I come with you? I would not disturb. I would bring my book."

"There's no question of disturbing, dear; but it would

be very boring for you. Why, what's happened? You said you didn't mind being alone."

"Until now I am *not* minding. In this house there is something that watches me—not kindly. I think that here I am not welcome. There is something wishes I did not come. It is not a good house to be alone in."

Kathy received this speech with mixed feelings. Maria's last sentence had a simplicity that emphasised its sinister meaning. But what a strange statement to come from one who so lately derided supernatural things as nonsense!

She said, "I know that feeling. I had it myself when I began to live alone. I must go because it's too late for them to find a fourth, but I'll ring Mrs. Broome and ask if you can go there."

"I will be grateful," Maria said humbly.

Mrs. Broome said heartily that in her household one more for supper wouldn't be noticeable; so Kathy left Maria at the big house on the outskirts of the town and drove on to Alice's, carrying with her the parcel containing two hundred and fifty copies of the quarterly bulletin of the Business and Professional Women's Club—Alice was the club's energetic secretary.

Alice took the parcel and said, "Do excuse me a minute. I want to glance at Dorothy's article about her Yugoslavian holiday. She writes such a foul hand I couldn't read her manuscript. How you can decipher such things beats me."

"Practice," Kathy said. "It's a good article. Often one types pretty automatically, but I found my attention arrested several times."

"I'll say you did," said Alice, leafing through the

bulletin's stapled pages. "Since when did page five come before four?"

"What?" Kathy cried with a note of dismay. "Oh, not again!"

She snatched a copy, saw it was paged wrongly, chose one from the centre of the pile—wrong again. Old Mrs. Coffle took a few to check. Every copy was wrong.

"Don't be so upset," Alice said. "It's not the end of the world."

"Why did you say, 'Oh, not again'?" Lucy Binder asked.

"Because it's the second time this week. And the other was just as mysterious. My new machine has a control which I set at the number of copies I want. I did a circular letter for the Theatre Fund; I set the control for two thousand, and, what is more, I used exactly four packets of paper that comes five hundred sheets to the packet. But Colonel Gregg rang me up in a fury and said I'd delivered only fifteen hundred copies. He had reason to be angry too; he had some helpers folding and putting the letters into addressed envelopes, and they had five hundred envelopes over, and I didn't get back till Saturday evening. I ran the extra ones off then and had them at his house by nine on Sunday morning, and I *offered* to help to fold them, but he looked at me as though I couldn't be trusted to do that properly."

"Alice," said Mrs. Coffle, "I think Kathy could do with a drink. And I know I could. Kathy, my dear, don't give them," she nodded towards the bulletins, "another thought. I still have the use of my hands, thank God. I'll pick 'em to pieces and put 'em together again tomorrow. It will give me something to do."

Kathy thanked her.

Alice, offering the drink, said, "I think you're over-working. Then you had to go and get yourself lumbered with that German girl."

"She's absolutely no trouble. In fact, she's a help now she's settled down. Considering the kind of life she's led, she's amazingly domesticated."

"How old is she?" Mrs. Coffle asked.

"Fifteen and a bit."

"Then she should be a help rather than a burden. Now, what about this game?"

Kathy knew that this was the moment when she should say that she wouldn't be able to play next week, or indeed again until Maria had overcome her dislike of being alone. She couldn't expect the Broomes to make a weekly thing of entertaining Maria, and if she brought her here to the Coffles' flat, there was no place really suitable for her to do her homework.

But she didn't mention the matter then, dreading the protests and persuasions of Mrs. Coffle, who had reached the stage where any change of routine was distasteful, because it hinted at life's impermanence. She'd ring up Alice and explain, early in the week, so that Alice could find a fourth player.

She rang up on Monday morning—always a slack time in a dress shop; and Alice received her explanation in what seemed a very casual manner. She said, "You could bring her with you, you know." When Kathy had explained the drawbacks to that, she said, "Well, you know best," and ended the conversation.

Going back to her work, Kathy thought dismally, *She's offended. I've lost a friend now!*

The work she was engaged upon—an auctioneer's catalogue—offered nothing to divert her gloomy trend of thought, and when the doorbell rang she was glad of the interruption. It was Colonel Gregg.

"Good morning, Mrs. Allbright," he said. "I've come in person to apologise."

"Oh, you found the other five hundred copies?" she asked eagerly.

"Good heavens, no! I didn't come to apologise for my arithmetic! But I felt I was a bit rude and hasty the other day; so, as I was passing, I thought that I would just look in and apologise for my language."

"That's very nice of you. I know it was annoying for you, and I didn't resent your language in the least."

They were by this time in her sitting-room, and as a sign of goodwill she reached for the silver box which always stood on top of her bookcase, intending to offer him a cigarette. As she turned towards him she opened the box, slammed it shut again, and dropped it. It fell into a chair. She felt her face go stiff. She wanted to scream and scream, give full vent to her horror and disgust, but some tiny remnant of sense restrained her. Colonel Gregg already thought she couldn't count; he must have no cause to think she was losing her sanity.

"Is anything wrong?" he asked.

"No. I just . . . excuse me a moment . . ." She hurried from the room and into the kitchen, where she leaned against the cold edge of the sink and retched without being sick. Then she washed her hands, feeling that to her they could never be clean again. You *must* pull yourself together, she told herself sternly, and made an effort, went to the cupboard, found a pack of cigarettes, and returned to the sitting-room.

"I'm sorry to have been so long. I mislaid my cigarettes." She opened the pack with fingers that felt boneless.

"You shouldn't have bothered," Colonel Gregg protested, but he accepted one with the foreseeable remark about a pipe of peace. As her cigarette wobbled in the flame of the match he held, he asked, "You sure you're all right? You've very shaky."

"I think it has turned cold. The Indian summer has gone, I'm afraid."

He said that women didn't wear enough clothes nowadays, and went rambling on, happily telling of his plans for further charitable appeals, threatening to keep her busy through the winter. She listened with what attention she could muster. Finally he left.

She went back to her workroom, and, because it was too late now for the relief of a screaming fit, cried and—as even not particularly religious people do in a crisis—called upon God. *O God help me! God what shall I do?* For this was an evil trick, aimed at her most vulnerable spot, motivated by a frightening malice.

Presently, when she was calmer, she examined the possibility that Maria might be responsible. But how account for Maria's dislike of being alone in the house? Pretence? Also, to have disposed of five hundred copies of Colonel Gregg's letter, to have switched the piles of pages of the bulletin, the girl must have been extremely quick, and lucky, since she had never, to Kathy's knowledge, been anywhere near the workroom.

It was horrible to suspect Maria; but the alternative—to suspect some supernatural agency—was worse.

When Maria returned from school, Kathy was in the kitchen, shakily drinking a cup of tea. Maria poured herself a glass of milk. She looked at Kathy and said, with concern, "You have been crying. You have bad news? You feel unwell?"

"No. I had a shock." The next words she had planned carefully, yet they seemed difficult to say. "Maria, I want you to do something for me."

"I will do whatever you say," Maria said.

"You know my silver cigarette box . . ." She paused deliberately and watched for any reaction.

"The one on the bookcase? Yes."

Maria neither blanched nor reddened or showed any other sign of guilty knowledge. Mentally, Kathy acquitted her before she went any further.

"A horrible thing happened this afternoon. I opened it and the cigarettes were gone and in it there was . . ." It must be said! "A dead frog."

"Oh, *nein! nein!*" Maria set the glass down clumsily, slopping some milk. "And this you wish me to remove? Is impossible. Aunt Kathy, even in a box I cannot touch one of *them!*"

Plainly innocent.

"I'll ask the postman, or the milkman," Kathy said, wishing that she had decided upon this course from the first, and said nothing to the girl.

"You opened it and found . . . If such thing had happened to me, I think I would die."

"I nearly did," Kathy said. "But I didn't intend to upset you, Maria. Forget about it. Drink your milk."

Maria moved her hands in a gesture of rejection. "I

am thinking," she said. "I think you are punished for bringing me here. Such things do not go in boxes and shut lids. The one to whom I am not welcome did this to you."

Fantastic, Kathy thought, but not more so than this afternoon's event.

"On me also tricks have been played. Not so nasty. Once there is writing in my book, and my best blouse cut with scissors."

"You never told me," Kathy said in a small, breathless voice.

"Partly I think you will mock me; partly I think you will upset yourself. So! Now it thinks it will begin on you."

"We mustn't jump to such conclusions, Maria. There must be some perfectly reasonable explanation."

"Tell me one. You see, you cannot. For me this house is bad, from the beginning. This I write to my father, and he says do not be fanciful. Now we will see what he says to this!"

A whole aspect, different, but appalling, sprang into being with the mention of Willi.

"Maria, *please,* don't bother him with a little thing like this. He'll think I'm out of my mind, making such a fuss. He'll think . . . Don't write, anyway until we've had a chance to think of some sensible explanation."

"He says I'm fanciful," Maria said. "I am not liking to be called fanciful. So! Tonight I give him the truth."

"For my sake, don't. Not tonight. Wait a little."

"You think," Maria said with relentless logic, "that tomorrow my blouse will be mended, and that thing will remove itself."

"No. I don't know what to think. I only know that it would be wrong, unkind, to worry your father just now."

"He is a man able to bear much worry; I write him that I am unhappy, that I am afraid; he says do not be fanciful. He is a man for facts. In the sitting-room is a fact, is it not?"

What could one answer? What could one do? Impossible to forbid the child to write to her father; impossible to write oneself and contradict. In the sitting-room was a fact. And facts must be faced.

She sat there, facing them, when a possible explanation flashed into her mind. Far-fetched, but there was some evidence; disturbing, but less so than the idea of a vague evil. A poltergeist!

Poltergeists were very often associated with girls in their early teens, especially with unhappy girls. A whole witch hunt had once started up around some repressed Puritan girls who were pricked by pins; there'd been a maid servant, in the attic-kitchen times, concerned with the manifestations at Borley Rectory. Poltergeists were comparatively harmless; people who would never say, "I have a ghost," would lightheartedly say, "There's a poltergeist in my house!" And though the trick played on her this afternoon was vicious and cruel, because of her phobia, to many people it would have been a mere puzzle, a joke, a typical poltergeistic trick.

She thought, *I can write to Willi along those lines.* She removed a stencil from her typewriter and inserted a clean sheet of paper.

"Dear Willi," she tapped out, "we seem to have acquired a poltergeist. . . ." She quoted other cases; she assured him that poltergeists were harmless; she explained the situation as something arising from Maria's homesickness. "In the old days they fastened on very unhappy girls, there are fewer of them nowadays, so being homesick was enough. . . ." When she had finished her letter and read it through, she was modestly pleased with its light, half-humorous touch. Whatever Maria had said, this should put Willi's mind at rest.

The postman kindly, but with some amusement, took the silver cigarette box and its contents. And then there was some waiting time. Kathy and Maria were both extremely cautious in opening the tea caddy, or the refrigerator. It was rather like advancing into enemy territory where the most ordinary object might conceal danger. But there were no further manifestations.

Then, one evening when Maria was doing her homework, the telephone rang and Kathy, picking up the receiver, heard the crisp voice of Maria's headmistress, Miss Clover.

It said, "Mrs. Allbright? Ah! I have just received a telegram from Mr. von Lodau. I gather that you know what it is about."

"No. I presume Maria."

"Maria, naturally . . . I imagined that you . . . Perhaps I had better read you what he says. I quote. 'Reasons health and sanity imperative Maria enters school as boarder. Please try accommodate. Situation most urgent. If accommodation impossible please find room in boding-house'—I think boarding house is there intended—'or hotel. Am contacting Mrs. Allbright.' Then there is the sender's name. Does that make sense to you, Mrs. Allbright?"

"Yes. In a way," Kathy said feebly.

"Well," the capable voice went on, "it is not our custom to take boarders except at the beginning of the term. But in an exceptional case we make concessions. Maria may bring her things and move in tomorrow. And I sincerely hope that you will soon be better."

With her conditioned politeness Kathy said, "Thank you," before replacing the receiver.

Now she felt boneless all over. *Willi thinks I'm mad,* she thought. *Willi thinks I'm affecting Maria. Miss Clover thinks I'm ill. How awful! How unfair!*

But almost immediately her thoughts shifted to Maria; poor child, doomed to spend evenings and days with the girls whose company she so despised.

Oddly enough, the idea of defying Willi and his decree never once occurred to her. She was old enough to remember the rules; men made decisions, women bowed to them. Fathers governed their children, and female relatives could never dream of opposing them.

"Am contacting Mrs. Allbright" meant that at any minute now the telephone might ring, or a young man on a motorcycle might arrive with a telegram and Maria must be prepared, and, if possible, comforted in advance.

She climbed the stairs and did what she had never yet done, opened the door behind which Maria was engaged with her homework.

Maria sat at the pretty little writing table for which Kathy had shopped so happily when thinking how nice it would be to have somebody young about the house; and she was reading, not writing. Kathy's eye, for more than a week now, sharpened, wary, alert, recognised the book even as Maria flattened it on the

table and placed her arms protectively over it, and
looked up, mildly and pleasantly questioning what this
interruption might mean. *The Most Haunted House in
England; Ten Years' Investigation of Borley Rectory.*

Complete comprehension swept over Kathy. The
whole thing was plain, from the evening when Maria had
said, about ghost stories, "And you are one of those?"
meaning a credulous person. And she stood there thinking, *I could forgive her, except for the box. She wanted
to get away from here and was willing to try anything.
She made the book about Borley her handbook. In
that dreadful house a dried reptile had been used as
an "apport," so, without thinking of its effect on me,
she used one; not dried but plump, repulsive, unforgettable. And she did that to me, though I had tried to
be kind to her, because she hoped that her father
would give in and order her to join him in Brazil. And
I, fool that I am, played along, wrote that silly letter,
so now Willi thinks I am mad.*

She stood there speechless. *I came to comfort her,*
she thought, *to prepare her for the message which is
now winging its way to us.*

Maria stared at her with those clear, innocent-looking
eyes and said, "Aunt Kathy, you are not well."

"No. I am not well." She doubted whether she
would ever feel completely well again. She'd been
aware of evil, had suspected it, but she had not
realised what it meant: sheer blind selfishness, prepared to go to any lengths to serve its own purposes.
"I'm going to bed."

"Can I get you anything?" The question was asked
with such eagerness and accompanied by a look of
such kind concern that Kathy thought of Judas.

"No, thank you."

"There is *nothing* I can do?"

"Yes. If the telephone rings, take a message; if a telegram comes, open it." Then she thought, *Oh, poor Maria,* and turned away to hide the tears.

Avoiding Dunstable

Accustomed to drinking with great moderation, but with fair regularity, Mr. Fairweather found it at first a little difficult to believe that he had slightly overdone it at his godson's wedding. The peculiar feeling which struck him when he had driven but ten miles of the seventy that he must cover, he attributed first to the practically sleepless night he had spent in the torture chamber which the bride's aunt called her guest room; and secondly to the inferior, indeed horrible champagne which the bride's father had provided for the reception. It was understandable, it was forgiveable; no honest man in these days could afford even moderately good champagne for four hundred guests, all drinking as though they had that moment emerged from the Sahara.

A bad night, a hurried and indigestible lunch; two, perhaps even three glasses of that acidulous beverage, accompanied by half a dozen mouthfuls of rubbishy nameless stuff, accounted easily, in Mr. Fairweather's logical mind, for the fact that he did not feel quite the thing. But, aware of the breathalyser laws, he drove very carefully indeed; and presently, as he did his careful driving, he remembered that before the hurried lunch he had drunk two glasses of tolerable sherry and that, as the bride and groom had departed amidst a flurry of confetti and paper rose petals, the bride's father had taken him aside and said, "Well, that's over. Let's you and me have a real drink." And that had been whisky, sound and good and at the time comforting.

Mr. Fairweather realised that he had committed the ultimate folly of mixing his drinks. And now, with tolerable sherry, bad champagne, and good whisky circulating in his blood he was out on the public highway, in charge of that lethal weapon, a motor-car.

The trouble was that the bride's aunt—a woman who knew everything except how to make an overnight guest comfortable—had told him how to cut his journey by at least fifteen miles. He was now on the road that she had advocated; a very narrow road, with no lay-by. So narrow, indeed, that once committed to it Mr. Fairweather had wondered what would happen should he meet another vehicle. Taking this road, he had realised within a few minutes, had been a weakness, a concession to his desire to avoid Dunstable, a town in which, driving up to the wedding, he had been—not lost, that he would never admit—but confused. Almost every signpost said "Whipsnade," and Whipsnade was not his destination. Dunstable, the bride's aunt had said, *could* be entirely avoided.

So now here he was, feeling not only somewhat intoxicated, but slightly unwell, on a narrow little road where it was impossible to turn round and dangerous to stop. And the day began to close down.

An overcast evening; perhaps in the circumstances wise to put sidelights on. He fiddled at the dashboard and the windscreen wipers began to clack. He turned them off, tried again, and a great stern voice, like God speaking from Sinai, came from the radio. At the third attempt he put his lights on.

Driving ability definitely impaired, thought Mr. Fairweather, who, as a solicitor, knew all the proper terms. He was also a J.P., and though his fingers had become clumsy his unimpaired imagination was active enough to foresee what the local paper would make of any misfortune that befell him. "Local J.P. charged with drunken driving." On the bench he was known for coming down pretty sharply on those who committed this offence.

He drove very slowly, very attentively, looking about for some break in the high, overhanging hedges. Had so much as a field gateway offered itself he would have gone in, stopped, and slept it off. But there was, for a long time, no opening at all. He had not felt so unwell since he suffered from influenza, nor so apprehensive since he stood outside his headmaster's door some forty years earlier. In such a rural district the policeman would undoubtedly ride a bicycle and as he crawled along Mr. Fairweather momentarily dreaded the appearance of this familiar and hitherto confidence-inspiring figure.

It was with great relief that he saw just ahead of him a board which said, in worn gold lettering: "The Grange. Residential Hotel. Open to non-residents." He turned in between the stone gateposts and drove for some distance along a drive whose weedy condition suggested that The Grange was not much patronised. And indeed the hotel was ill placed. Since leaving the main road Mr. Fairweather had not seen another car, nor anyone on foot. He brought his car to a standstill between the house and an enormous dark cedar tree, and thankfully closed his eyes, which were not focusing well. Shutting his eyes increased his dizziness. So he opened them again and studied, with deliberate concentration, as much of the house as he could see.

It was not prepossessing. Victorian Gothic, built at a time when money was plentiful, taste at its lowest ebb. Mr. Fairweather himself owned a very elegant small Georgian town house and withheld admiration from anything built after 1830. Still, he knew that any bedroom in this house was capable of holding a full-size bed, and that, after a night in a room roughly nine feet by six, on a divan bed three feet wide and rather less than six feet long, was his most pressing requirement at present.

He turned off the car lights and got out and moved to the door, pleased to find that he was neither weaving nor reeling—two of the favourite accusative words. Now that the sun had gone down, the late evening was chilly, refreshing; he took several deep breaths of it before pushing open the door and entering the hotel where, if anything, it was even more chilly.

Except for the fact that a handsome library table

stood at right angles to the door and bore an open book for registration, a bus and a railway timetable and a few brochures, there was nothing to distingush this from a private dwelling, the "lounge-hall" of a country house that was the favourite setting for plays in the thirties. There were some comfortable-looking chairs and sofas with faded chintz covers, and, mounded up directly under the predictable skylight in the centre, a collection of plants which, recently watered, gave off an earthy scent which mingled agreeably with those of furniture or floor polish and something cooking. To the left an uncarpeted but well-polished staircase of pine led off to the upper floor, lost in obscurity because the hall was ill lit.

On the library table stood a brass bell against which was lodged a slip of cardboard bearing the words "Please Ring." Mr. Fairweather smote it sharply.

As the bell pinged, more or less committing him, he realised that, given a little time to recover himself, he could perfectly well have driven home. He had, in fact, succumbed to that reasonless fear which made people drive on after they had knocked down a child . . . or even attempt to dispose of dead bodies. "Well. I knew everybody'd blame me. So I got in a panic."

Mr. Fairweather had gone all through the war; North Africa, tanks. He had momentarily expected to be killed, wounded, or captured, possibilities that he had accepted and therefore never regarded as reason for panic. He had a decoration; he was entitled to call himself *Colonel* as many men did, but, a purist, he despised the custom. The truth was that Rommel had never inspired in him anything like such panic as had, so short time ago, come upon him when he thought of the village constable, on a bicycle.

In response to the bell's call a door somewhere within the deep shadow of the staircase opened, a man came out. So did the cooking smell. Knitting itself into Mr. Fairweather's suvey of the "lounge-hall," his awareness of a kind of amateurness, had been the expectation that whoever answered the bell would be either a slightly drooping lady—turning the family home into a hotel to make ends meet—or a vastly moustachioed hail-fellow-well-met ex-R.A.F. type running a hotel to supplement his pension.

But the man who came, switching on three more of the candle lights in the hideous travesty of a chandelier, was something different. Something for which Mr. Fairweather was not prepared. A large, rather sombre man wearing a dark, antiquated suit.

He said: "Good evening, sir."

"Good evening. I should like a room—if you have it, one with a double bed and private bathroom." That morning—it now seemed quite a long time ago—Mr. Fairweather had been unable to get into the bathroom, even for the most necessary purpose, because the bride's aunt had also offered hospitality to the groom and the best man and they had spent what seemed to be hours taking baths.

The man said: "If you would come this way, sir."

Mr. Fairweather looked first at the bed. A big double bed, wide enough, long enough.

"The bathroom, sir."

"It will do very well," Mr. Fairweather said.

"Then I will have your bag brought in and your car put into the garage. You wish to take dinner, sir?"

Mr. Fairweather's stomach, not yet quite resigned to the maltreatment it had suffered, made a mild protest;

but his head was wiser. A good solid meal was what he needed.

The man said: "We cannot offer a varied menu, sir. We decided that one carefully chosen, well-cooked meal was preferable—and more to the taste of gentlemen."

"I agree," Mr. Fairweather said. But he also thought, that is now a dirty word. There are no gentlemen—there are members of an upper income group . . . not the same thing at all.

"Consommé, saddle of mutton, and gooseberry tart with cream," the man said.

Mr. Fairweather's stomach abandoned its protests.

The dining-room, capable of seating thirty at least, was empty but for himself. The man who had received him and shown him the room now waited upon him, deft-handed, soft-footed, and in silence until, placing the succulent meat before him, he asked if Mr. Fairweather would care for a glass of Burgundy. "We do not carry a wine-list, sir, but our Burgundy is good."

It—and indeed the whole meal—was so good, the napery and silver so superior and the service so commendable that Mr. Fairweather was astonished that the place was not crowded. It was badly placed; but he remembered the saying that if a man made a better mousetrap than the average, the world would beat a way to his door even if he lived in the middle of a forest. He knew that were The Grange within ten miles of his home, he would dine there every evening.

At the end, touching his lips with the table napkin so well starched and glossy, he said: "The best meal I have had for many a long day."

"Thank you, sir."

"Am I to be the only one to take advantage of it?"

"I am afraid so, sir. We are a little off the beaten track."

"So I thought. But word must get around . . ."

"Unfavourable more often than not," the man said. "What we have to offer is not much appreciated these days. It is indeed a very long time since I had the pleasure of attending a gentleman like yourself, sir."

Mr. Fairweather was not flattered by this remark. He knew his own worth.

Now, fully restored by his meal and the excellent wine, he had regained his usual genial temper and with it his professional interest in other people's business. He looked more closely at the man and saw that, though neat and clean, his old-fashioned clothes were shabby and that he had the somewhat collapsed look of one who in his time had carried much more weight. It was the empty folds of what had been a full-fleshed face that gave him that melancholy look.

"It can hardly be a paying proposition," he said, with just that touch of casualness that made the remark inoffensive.

"It never has been," the man admitted. "A few, at first, prompted by curiosity. And of course the overheads are heavy."

"How large a staff?"

"Lately only myself, sir."

"What! You mean you cook? And clean and . . . and everything?"

"That is so. With so few customers the work is not onerous."

At the very back of Mr. Fairweather's mind a little thought began to bud. The man was obviously wasted here. And how well, how superbly well, he would fit into the elegant little Georgian house! Mr. Fairweather, until six years before, had had a cook-housekeeper, a veritable treasure; he had expected to keep her for ever and had made provision for her in his will. But the moment she was eligible for a pension she had retired, with hurtful alacrity, to live with a sister. He now employed a cheerful sloven who came each morning, made some execrable coffee, burned some toast and misused an egg or two, made his bed, flapped about with a duster, and having set out a pork pie or a few slices of ham for his evening consumption, went home. If only . . .

But it was impossible to make the suggestion until he had investigated the circumstances.

"To whom does this place belong?" he asked.

"To me, sir."

This certainly was an evening of surprises. "It was left to me," the man explained, "by my late master, Mr. Dunton. I had been with him for over thirty years." The look of melancholy deepened. "He had no relatives. He left everything to me. Unfortunately, though nobody knew, even I myself did not know, Mr. Dunton had suffered financial reverses and had been living on his capital for some time. When the estate was settled there was almost nothing except the house."

"A white elephant. Did you ever attempt to dispose of it?"

"No. I am certain that that would not have been in accord with Mr. Dunton's wishes, sir. Mr. Dunton was a gentleman who was . . . was accustomed to having his own way. And although he never gave me a direct order in this regard, I was so accustomed to interpreting, even forestalling his wishes, I know what he wished. Such knowledge has been a handicap in other ways, too. He would have been against any attempt to make the place popular. In fact, I have never served a meal here of which Mr. Dunton himself would not approve; nor do I extend a warm welcome to anyone whom Mr. Dunton would not wish to receive under his roof."

"But that is no way to run a business!"

"So it would seem, sir."

"I think," Mr. Fairweather said, "that your loyalty, while highly creditable, highly, has been overdone. It verges, if I may say so, upon the sentimental. It would not be an easy house to dispose of; but as a school, or a nursing home . . ."

"Offers have been made. But I know how Mr. Dunton . . . And if that is sentimental and should be ignored, there is a practical aspect. I should then be without a roof."

"Good God, man!" said Mr. Fairweather who seldom took his Maker's name in vain. "A man like you! You'd be killed in the rush. Why, I myself—I have a small, manageable house in the very centre of a pleasant market town. It has every modern amenity. I have daily help. I could pay you . . ." He did a swift sum. "Eight hundred pounds a year."

"It sounds attractive," the man said. For a moment he seemed to think seriously about it, working his big, thin, very clean hands together. Mr. Fairweather allowed himself one, just one, greatly daring peep into the future; imagine being able to entertain at home once more! Imagine coming back in the evening!

"I'm sorry, sir. I am indeed *very* sorry. But I am sure that it would be against Mr. Dunton's wishes. I know as well as though he had told me himself, that he wishes me to remain here."

"I think you're a fool," Mr. Fairweather said, a little sharply because tomorrow and tomorrow the pork pie and the sliced ham would alternate, paving a savourless path to the grave.

"You are not alone in that opinion, sir," the man said. "Is there anything further I can get you?"

"No, thank you. I've had a tiring day and must make an early start. I'll turn in."

He looked at his watch. It was just on ten o'clock.

"Goodnight, sir. I trust you sleep well."

"You think over what I have said," Mr. Fairweather said, putting on the face petty offenders knew. "Goodnight."

The hall, as he crossed it, was very cold, so was his bedroom. But his bag had been brought in and opened. His pyjamas and dressing-gown lay on the bed, and in the bathroom even his toothbrush had been assigned a place. Shivering a little he slipped into bed and discovered a hot-water bottle in a pink flannel cover. He arranged himself in the area already warmed and clutching the bottle to his stomach drifted towards sleep. He hoped that the man—he should have asked his name—*was* thinking things over.

He woke to pain; to quite the worst headache he had suffered since the morning after the Oxford and Cambridge Boat Race. He half opened his eyes and then closed them against the stabbing light. Who, he wondered, had drawn the curtains? The pain was not confined to his head; he ached all over, every limb, every joint. He had a savage crick in his neck. He thought muzzily—So it was 'flu! I did not drive under the influence of alcohol after all.

He then realised that he was in his car, his head on the steering wheel. He straightened himself, pressed his hands to his eyes, and looked out over what appeared to be a field of sugar beet, young leaves shining in the level rays of the early morning sun.

Only one explanation seemed possible. The man, who must be slightly mad, had decided that after all he was not fit to sleep under Mr. Dunton's roof, had carried him out and crammed him into the car.

He got out, stretched his cramped limbs, and stood rubbing his neck. He was not within sight of the house, nor of the cedar tree, so tall a tree as to be a landmark from a considerable distance. So he had been put into his car and driven into the sugar beet field.

As the congestion in his head eased, the pain ebbed, and his mental processes quickened. It was a fantastic thing to have happened to *him,* of all people, but he suspected that he had stumbled upon something mysterious, perhaps even criminal. The man's story, now that he came to examine it, was palpably untrue—running a huge house like that single-handed; cooking a whole saddle of lamb on the chance that some guest would arrive.

Besides such aspects of crime as he was professionally concerned with, he was familiar with others more colourful and exciting.

He remembered the chill in the house, as though it were long unused; and the extreme quietude, less an absence of noise than a positive silence. He could imagine that behind that softly swinging door breath had been held, whispered words spoken. "That damned board," one would say; "should have taken it down. Go on, Bob, head them off. Make up some tale."

Alone, carefully backing out of the field, Mr. Fairweather felt embarrassed, and coloured when he thought of the tale with which he had been fobbed off and which he had accepted. Offering the man a job!

As he drove along the narrow lane he kept a sharp look out for the board, the gateposts. Since he did not see them he decided that whoever had dumped him had driven in the direction he was now taking and that the house lay behind him. He drove fast and in a few minutes came, as the bride's aunt had promised, to Webfield, where he would rejoin the main road, having avoided Dunstable.

In the village he began looking for a police station. It was easily found, fronted by a board to which was tacked a photograph under the word "wanted" and some directions as to how to recognise a Colorado beetle and what to do when you recognise it.

The constable himself answered the door, a nice-looking young man. He was in his shirt sleeves. Through an open door behind him Mr. Fairweather saw a breakfast table; the wife, two children.

"I'm sorry to disturb you at breakfast," Mr. Fairweather said. "But I think I should . . . well, not report exactly, but tell you something."

"That's all right, sir. I'd just finished. Come in please. I'll just . . ." but his wife, like a well-trained retriever, was already holding the blue jacket at the ready. The constable slipped into it, buttoned it, and smoothed it down.

Mr. Fairweather realised that in his creased suit,

and unshaven, he did not present a very respectable appearance. So he fumbled out a card and offered it.

"Yes, sir?" the constable invited.

"I may be quite wrong," Mr. Fairweather began. "But last night I had a very curious experience—as you will agree, when you hear. I think the circumstances warrant investigation. I am not suggesting that you should go alone," he put in, remembering the wife, the children. "I saw only one man, but I have come to the conclusion that he had companions. After all, a whole saddle of mutton . . . And let us be clear on this point, I am not lodging a complaint. No harm was done me. On the contrary, I had a free dinner. But I have always held that if people reported any peculiar behaviour a great deal of crime could be prevented."

The constable was accustomed to dealing with people either congenitally or temporarily incapable of coherence, so he said patiently: "If you could begin at the beginning, sir."

"Of course," Mr. Fairweather said. He also had in his time suffered under the incoherent. "I am not quite myself this morning. To go to sleep in a bed and to wake in a car in a field of sugar beet is not exactly conducive to lucidity. I assume that you know the side road, nothing more than a lane, which runs between this village and the next?"

"Very well," said the constable, who cycled along it at least once a day.

"Last evening, on that road," Mr. Fairweather began. Once launched the story became concise and detailed. He withheld the true reason for breaking his journey where he did, attributing his action to a sleepless night and a tiring day. He also forebore to mention that he had offered the man employment—that was an irrelevance.

As he spoke he watched the young fresh-coloured face, half expecting some sign of scepticism; for related like this the tale sounded almost incredible. There was no such sign, but the face did change a little, so slightly that only one accustomed to watching closely would have noticed it. There was a faint lessening of colour around the nostrils, a faint clouding of the candid blue eyes. As though the man were suffering some embarrassment. It was the look some men wore when they were forced to listen to a risqué story.

The reason for his embarrassment was revealed when he spoke. "Excuse me, sir, may I ask one question? You were sober when you parked your car?"

"Yes," said Mr. Fairweather, now convinced of this himself. "I can offer evidence of that. The drive is thickly overgrown with weeds. My car must have left tracks which will show that I drove straightly and parked with precision between the main doorway and the cedar tree." He thought that over for a second and saw its weakness. "Naturally I cannot answer for the driver who later took my car into the field. My tracks may be obscured."

The embarrassed look deepened.

"Of course, sir. I just wondered, because a slight, very slight degree of intoxication seemed to me to be a possible alternative."

"Alternative to what?"

"I don't know. What I do know is that there is no house such as you describe in that particular lane. There *was*," he said, forestalling Mr. Fairweather's protest. "And it was called The Grange and it was a hotel for a while. Long before my time. I've only been here three years, but I married a local girl. The Grange was demolished, ploughed over, sir. About twelve years ago."

"Obviously," Mr. Fairweather said crisply, "we are not speaking about the same place. Grange after all is a very usual name. If you will come with me I will show you the one I mean."

"There is no other Grange around here, sir. If there was, and if it had ever been a hotel, I should know, because of the licensing. And the sugar beet means something to me. I always take note of that crop; good cover for pheasants and partridges, and we have our share of poachers. This year the field that now incorporates the site of The Grange, its garden, orchard, and paddock, *is* under sugar beet."

"Good God!" Mr. Fairweather said again. "Are you trying to tell me that I dined and went to bed in a nonexistent house?"

"I don't know. I try not to think about what I can't understand. And I never tell my wife if I have to go along that road after dark; she'd worry. But I do go, and I've never seen, or heard or smelled anything. But some have; and Mr. Stutton—he's the farmer who took over and pulled the house down—has had trouble. Nobody will work in that field by himself, or run a tractor or a combine harvester—it was barley last year —after dusk, never mind the overtime. They look on it"—by now the young policeman's colour was concentrated into two almost circular patches under his eyes—"as haunted," he said, bringing out the word with reluctance.

Mr. Fairweather was equally reluctant to accept it.

He said almost pettishly, "I find this hard to believe. I'm the last man in the world . . ." Almost feverishly searching for some fingerhold on the ordinary, he remembered that in telling his story he had mentioned no name. "When the house stood, to whom did it belong?"

"To a Mr. Dunton."

"Yes," Mr. Fairweather said in a voice unlike his own, "that was the name. What . . . what happened to him?"

"I only know what my wife has told me; and I don't encourage her to talk about it. But her mother worked there at one time. So naturally . . . Mr. Dunton seemed to grow miserly, the way old people often do. He sacked everybody except this one man—Baxter his name was—but he still expected to be looked after properly. He used to read in bed, with a candle to save electricity, and one night he set his bed on fire. Well, sir, you know what gossip is; what with his having used Baxter so hard and having left him all he had, there was a lot of talk. All he had sounded a lot but what it boiled down to was the property and a few hundred pounds."

"Exactly as I was told. And then?"

"He tried to run it as a hotel, but he had a manner that put people off, staff and customers. And there was a bad winter, 1947 I think. The lane was blocked, and the drive. When they got through to him he was dead. Everybody around here said that it was a judgment on him."

Mr. Fairweather found himself, for the first time in his adult life, speechless.

"It's odd," the policeman said, reflectively. "So far as I know nobody else ever saw or heard anything out of the way. Always smells; always food; toast, fried bacon, joints roasting. In the middle of a field. In broad daylight."

The bleak little room, the telephone, the posters, the solid young policeman, the whole solid world in which for half a century Mr. Fairweather had felt at home wavered and splintered and he saw for a moment infinite space, infinite time—concepts that few men could consider and remain sane. In that moment he did not give the proper consideration to guilt or innocence.

He saw the wronged dominant entity taking an endless vengeance and the one who had done the wrong . . . impatient, weary, perhaps hungry, doomed to serve phantom meals, pour phantom wine for phantom gentlemen, through all eternity. Not a life sentence; not a death sentence. For ever. And for ever.

He knew that for him life would never be quite the same again; but that was neither here nor there. Every man must bear his own burden of consciousness, make his own compromise.

"I think, constable," Mr. Fairweather said, "the less said about it the better."

"So I think, sir. There's enough to cope with with what you can understand, more or less, and try to deal with. To be honest, I never paid much attention to the tales. But this, coming from a gentleman like yourself, sir . . ."

Echo responded to echo, and for one dreadful moment Mr. Fairweather saw before him not the youthful face and trim blue uniform but the sad, jowled face and the seedy black—uniform too, in its

way, in its time. Which was real? Am I real? Consider
Time divorced from clocks and calendars, and Space as
something unconfined by walls, and one might well ask
oneself, what is real?

A Clinical Case

I began to get fat when I was twelve. Mother said
briskly, "No more starchy food, my girl. You'll soon
fine down." She flung herself into the business of dieting
me with her usual efficiency; but without her usual
success. She bought books and charts, cut articles from
papers. I followed all the directions conscientiously,
and continued to fatten. Mother does not take defeat
easily; we began a round of doctors; there was talk of
calories, of puppy fat, of glandular deficiency, of in-
cipient diabetes. There was nothing in my physical
condition, everyone assured us, to account for my bulk.
And there was no need to worry. "But I do. Wouldn't

you, if *you* had a daughter who lived for a week on green salad, without dressing, and drank two cups of *black* coffee a day and *gained a pound?"*

She fretted about it so much that after a time I pretended not to care: but I did, passionately. Clothes became a problem; the jeans and mini-skirts that were fashionable that year were impossible wear for me: in an ordinary woollen pullover Mother said, quite rightly, that I looked disgusting, and the thick fisher-knit jerseys, though kinder to the outline, simply added to my bulk. I spent my days in skirts and blouses either altered to fit or made specially for me by the clever little dressmaker whom Mother employed in her shop. There were other disadvantages as well; I had been a promising tennis player; I still played a good game and was speedier than might have been expected, but I did not get into the school team. I knew why: I looked so horrible, floundering about the court in a skirt just long enough to cover my bulbous knees and the blubber on my arms quivering. I gave up parties too, who wants to dance with a fat girl? I took to long, solitary walks, read a great deal, and studied hard. That year I won three prizes, English, History, Maths, but under my tread the steps and the platform creaked as I went to collect my awards; and had I allowed myself to I should have wept with mortification.

One blow remained to fall. Mother said, "Really, Sally, I think you had better keep out of the shop. It's such a bad advertisement."

"You mean people may be afraid to buy one of Mrs. Hayter's frocks for fear they grow like Mrs. Hayter's daughter?"

She gave me the look, half-wary, half-reproachful,

that she always shot at me when I made a remark of that kind.

"You know very well what I mean," she said. "And there's no need to be sarcastic. It's not my fault."

Being banned from the shop was a real deprivation. It had always seemed to me to be the centre of beauty and elegance and luxury. My father had died young and Mother, with herself and me, a child of four to support, had seen, as she often said, that what our town needed was something different. She supplied it. Champton is an ugly town, expanding fast and very prosperous, full of square new factories and square new houses and the square new shops, almost all branches of big multiple stores. Mother bought one of the few old houses that remained over from the original village; had a few walls knocked down, so that the ground floor became one spacious room; the old panelled walls were painted white, the floor carpeted in dull rose. The light fell from chandeliers—modern, but effective imitations—and from matching fitments on the walls. The clothes were not on display. In the bay window there was always one especially attractive frock, suit, hat, or fur, and great lavish flower display. Inside, over the bogus Louis Quinze sofa another selected garment might lie, as though casually discarded. And against the far wall there was always another flower arrangement. "It was a gamble," Mother often said, "but it paid off." There had been a period of touch-and-go, and then the wives of the factory owners and the executives and of ambitious men in minor positions, most of whom had formerly bought their clothes in London, discovered that to be well-dressed one must go to Mrs. Hayter. And presently, not only for clothes. For a reasonable rake-off Mother would house-and sell a piece of furniture, a picture, a necklace. She had, in addition, established the nearest thing to a salon that the twentieth century permits. If you were fitting a suit at Mrs. Hayter's around eleven o'clock in the morning you were offered coffee; at four in the afternoon, tea; and over these beverages you might meet almost anyone. There was also an element of exchange and mart, because everybody confided in Mrs. Hayter. Mrs. X wished to get rid of her au pair girl—very flighty; Mrs. Y, married to a man with whom no au pair girl could possibly get flighty, only too thankfully took the girl on. There was a similar trade in jobbing gardeners, self-employed plumbers, electricians, carpenters. And there was a pathetic side to it, too. Every now and then, a woman, out of her depths, buying a dress for an important occasion, buying an outfit for a daughter about to be a bride would ask, obliquely, for a little social guidance. "I do want everything to be nice, Mrs. Hayter." Mother always saw to it that everything was nice. I must give her her due; she would go to endless pains; and people were grateful and faithful. When the time came for the buying of the new mink coat or the library bookcase, most of them remembered Mrs. Hayter who had told them how to word a wedding invitation, or seat people at a dinner party. She never betrayed a confidence, she never gossiped, she never faltered, and she never failed.

But no woman can expend more than a certain amount of enterprise and energy; our home life was bleak. Above the shop and the workrooms and the fitting rooms, we lived in a close-handed flat made out of what had been servants' quarters. There was no clutter, Mother would not have tolerated that; there was equally no comfort, no beauty. All that I had ever known of what they call "gracious living" had always been concentrated downstairs, in the shop.

Presently I was fifteen. I had taken my O-levels and knew that if marks were fairly given I had at least eight safely in the bag; the long, dull summer holiday loomed. And then somebody told Mother of a wonderful place, a kind of clinic where, under one roof, every known method for stripping unwanted flesh from overladen bones was employed.

Newtonford was a long way from Champton and in very different country, gently rolling, sparsely populated. The village lay in a little dip, the Clinic, which had once been the manor house, stood higher.

I was the only patient under forty and though I was kindly received I was conscious that even here I was regarded as a bit of a freak. "Well," one fat old man said to me genially, "in your case they can't blame business lunches, can they?"

You began by having nothing but fruit juice for three days. My weight stayed steady and the doctor to whom I had been assigned said, "Are you sure you haven't been eating on the sly? Don't hesitate to tell me. Most people do." He was young and rather handsome in a craggy way and I would not have tricked him or lied to him for anything in the world. I said, "No. How could I? I haven't been outside the grounds." On the fruit-juice days you were not supposed to walk much; but most patients had cars; some had chauffeurs, too.

"Well, don't be discouraged," Dr. Martin said. "We've never had a failure yet." He put me on the green vegetable diet; spinach, lettuce, grated cabbage. I gained a pound.

"We can't go on *starving* you," Dr. Martin said. "You must be very hungry."

I said, "Don't worry about that. I'm used to it. I've been hungry more or less for three years."

"We mustn't despair," he said.

Dieting was not, of course, the whole of it; there was a kind of Turkish bath in which you sweated like a pig; there were all kinds of exercises, hard-handed people who massaged, and underwater massage which is much less pleasant than it sounds—like being hosed down by the police if you are a street demonstrator, except that you can't run away. But nothing served for me. At the end of ten days at Newtonford I weighed exactly the same as I had when I arrived.

"You really are a very stubborn case," Dr. Martin said. "But we must not give in. Any day now you will begin to lose weight and then it will come down with a rush."

Mrs. Macer said the same. She was the one person there with whom I was on slightly more than speaking terms. She could read. We talked about books, and about weight. Newtonford had done wonders for her. On my tenth day she was ready to leave, her skin and her clothes sagging, she had lost twenty-nine pounds.

When she said good-bye to me she fumbled in her handbag and took out a little bottle. She said, "Dearie, any day now you will begin to lose weight and then it will come down with a rush. Like me. But . . . well it's a bit much to go into . . . a friend of mine, a very dear friend, when he heard I was coming here gave me these and said if nothing else worked, these would. But I'm all right now. So you have them. . . ."

She pressed the bottle into my hand, gave me a Chanel 5 scented kiss, and went towards her car where her chauffeur held the door open.

"One a day, dearie," she said.

Once off the fruit-juice régime, you were allowed, indeed encouraged to walk. I had walked a good deal, always avoiding the road that led down towards the village, climbing the slope behind the Clinic and then branching off, this way and that, over the sheep-nibbled, thyme-scented grass. I called it, to myself, Brontë country; I had never seen a Yorkshire moor.

On the afternoon of Mrs. Macer's departure I set out as usual intending to walk a little and then flop down and read: but I felt more vigorous than usual, perhaps because I was now on meat-and-fish, all grilled. I went uphill and then down and found a place that I had never reached before. There was a red wall of the kind sometimes called a ribbon wall, sometimes a crinkle-crankle; made of narrow reddish-pinkish bricks and with a gateway. I peeped in. It was a garden, rather formal; paved paths, some sharply clipped yews and rose *trees,* trees, rearing up, stripped stems like broom handles and then bursting out, umbrella-like, into a shower of bloom; red and pink, yellow and white, orange and cream. I had never seen anything like it.

While I was staring a girl came out from one of the inner curves of the winding wall. She was about my age, but very slim and pretty. She was eating a plum, yellow and red, dripping with juice. She wiped the back of her hand across her mouth and said, "Hullo. Do you want Madame?"

I said, "No . . . I was just admiring the garden. I have never seen such roses. . . ."

The girl said, "Most of them from Malmaison. Come in and take a proper look. What's your name?"

"Sally Hayter."

"I'm Marie," she said—and that made me feel silly for having given my full name. Her manner was easy and friendly and she seemed to take my gross appearance as a natural thing, neither staring nor obviously averting her eyes—the usual reactions. "We'll go round," she said, avoiding the path; "I find grass easier to walk on." As soon as we began to move I understood why; she walked with a pronounced limp. And that, I thought, probably accounts for her acceptance of me, perhaps she has been regarded with curiosity and pity.

In each curve of the wall there was a fruit tree, plums, apricots, pears, and apples. Marie plucked another plum and said, "Help yourself."

"I'm supposed to be on a diet," I said.

"Break out for once. Be a devil!" she said. And what was the diet doing for me, anyway? I ate four plums and three apricots as we walked. By that time we were near the house, a long low building made of the same bricks as the wall. From somewhere within or behind it came the sound of voices—young—and a good deal of laughter. I stopped.

"I think I'd better go back now."

"But you haven't seen half! There's a fountain. And a maze. Besides, you must meet Madame. You'll like her."

We rounded the corner of the house and there, on the far side, was the most wonderful fountain; a great stone-encircled pool, in the centre of which three stone horses reared. Water gushed from their mouths and splashed into the pool, sending up jets of spray which in the sunshine shone with rainbow colours. In the pool, laughing as they plunged and pushed one another under the gushing water and screaming with delight and mock terror, were six or seven young people, scantily clad.

"I'm not allowed to do *that* yet," Marie remarked. "I've had polio. I may swim, but I mustn't be jostled. Colin—the one in the red slip—is inclined to jostle when he gets excited."

They all looked to me to be between twelve and fifteen—too closely of an age to be one family.

"Is it a school?" I asked.

"Kind of. We're all backward." I suppose I looked astonished. "Oh, I don't mean dull-witted or simple. We've all been ill or delicate or something, and missed a lot of lessons; so we come here to make up. Colin was in a car smash; they say he was in a coma for three weeks; even now he's only allowed to work for an hour a day." She turned towards some steps that led downwards. "The maze is down here."

"Ought you to walk any more?" I asked.

"Oh yes. Walking is good for me."

I had read about mazes, but I had never seen one.

Marie said, "I won't come in with you. It's more fun alone. But if you get tired of it just call and I'll direct you."

I was lucky, I suppose; I only took the wrong turning twice. Marie seemed much impressed; most people took half an hour at least and some never mastered it at all. We climbed back on to the wide terrace where the fountain was, and there, between the fountain and the house, stood a woman, indubitably Madame, and Dr. Martin from the Clinic.

Marie made the introductions with aplomb. Madame Barthou shook hands with me and smiled; Dr. Martin said, "Sally and I are old friends."

Madame was about the age of my mother and not unlike her in figure and carriage, but her hair and eyes were black.

"Sally is frightfully clever," Marie said. "She did the maze in seven minutes flat."

"I've always thought that Sally had her wits about her," Dr. Martin said.

Madame Barthou said, rather drily, "I hope you will come often, Sally. Some intelligence would be useful around here at times."

"Oh Madame!" Marie protested, laughing. "We're not unintelligent, we're just backward!"

"And lazy also. And now it is time for tea. You will both stay?"

Dr. Martin said thank you, no; he must get back. I imagined the joy of walking beside him over the thyme-scented grass, and having something to talk about besides what I weighed; so I began to proffer my own cast-iron excuse for refusing invitations to tea. He broke in, however, and said, "You stay. Some young company is just what you need. Do you the world of good."

"But if I mustn't eat . . ."

He looked at me closely and said, "I do believe you're improving. Yes, definitely. You may have some tea. I wouldn't advise cake."

It was three years since I had eaten fresh, white, spongy bread and I have never eaten, and never shall eat, anything so delicious as Madame Barthou's sandwiches; cream cheese mixed with chopped chives, egg, sardine. I confined myself to one of each—thinking that I should pay for this tomorrow. But I did enjoy myself. The other boys and girls seemed to be as friendly and accepting as Marie; and for the first time it dawned on me that there were worse things in the world than a surplus of flesh. One girl named Betty, quite extraordinarily beautiful, had had one eye removed. "To save the other," she explained. She and Marie and a boy called Timothy walked with me to the gate when I left, and we all said, "See you tomorrow." I seemed to float back to the Clinic.

And plainly things had taken a turn for the better with me. At the weighing in the next morning I was eleven ounces lighter.

"You were right, you see, Dr. Martin," I said happily.

"Yes. I told you we'd never had a failure yet," he said.

Actually I was remembering not that remark, made some days earlier, in a pretty impersonal manner, but what he had said on the terrace the previous afternoon—definitely improving. He seemed to have forgotten that.

I said, "I was very careful, considering the temptation. And of course you didn't know that I'd already eaten four plums and three apricots. Perhaps I should have told you."

He gave me what I thought was a peculiar look.

"Yes; you should have mentioned it. In future . . .
However, no harm done."

I did my stint of exercise in the gymnasium; had
my underwater massage and the rest after it. I ate my
lunch, grilled steak and a plate of watercress, and then
set out for Madame Barthou's. I had no feeling that I
was imposing myself; Madame Barthou had herself said
that I must come often and I intended, this afternoon,
to help Timothy with his Maths. He was twelve, faced
with an examination called Common Entrance which
would admit him to a Public School; but he had a burst
appendix which had developed into peritonitis and was
badly behind with Maths.

It was, down in Newtonford, just such a sunny afternoon as yesterday's; but when I had climbed the slope
behind the Clinic, and gone down the slope into the
next dip, drifts of mist began. At first they didn't bother
me much; I have a good sense of direction. But it was
not like being in a street, or on a road, or even in a
maze; in that open country, with no landmarks, you
just wander in circles. I tried not to get into a panic,
but I was frightened: and cold too. My cotton blouse
and skirt clung to me clammily and the fog moisture
dripped from my hair into my eyes. It was sheer luck
that as I struggled to the top of another slope the fog
cleared and there below me lay the Clinic.

In the morning I weighed almost a pound less.

"Quite dramatic," Dr. Martin said. He sounded
pleased. I thought how pleased Mother would be, too.
I thought of having new clothes, of being back in the
tennis team. It was like being restored to life.

That afternoon I set off for Madame Barthou's and

there was no fog. They all seemed pleased to see me: I helped Timothy with his Maths—he was more than backward, and so felt that I had earned my tea. But again I was careful, eating only two sandwiches. Naturally I explained about the previous afternoon; they had had no fog there, they said. By this time we were on such friendly terms that I could talk about the Clinic, making it sound a good deal more comic than it actually was; for there is something pathetic as well as amusing in having a place called the Bar, with a proper-looking barman serving little glasses of carrot or celery juice. When I spoke about the underwater massage Colin said, "You see, Betty, people *pay* to be shoved into the spray. I do it for you free and you just scream." It was all so merry and light-hearted. Madame Barthou even remembered what I had said about being lost in the fog.

"It must have been very unpleasant. To come by the road is better, and not much farther. Seldom is there fog on the road."

Oddly enough, I had never thought of this house having any approach except from the way which I had discovered. But of course it had; it was linked to Newtonford village by a side road that branched off by the post office. Remembering my fright of yesterday I decided to take that way home.

However, that was not necessary because just as I was thinking of leaving Dr. Martin arrived. Marie, Betty, Colin, and I played a game of Scrabble while he talked to Madame Barthou and looked at those who were still under medical supervision, and drank a glass of sherry. Then we set out together, taking the way across open country. The springy turf felt and smelt just as I imagined it would do in such company and the talk was easy, free, and friendly; mainly about Madame Barthou and her pupils. Dr. Martin seemed to admire her as much as I did: she had, he said, the knack of restoring people's confidence.

"And making them happy," I said. "It is the happiest place I have ever seen."

"And strictly speaking," he said, "it shouldn't be. They're all rather pitiable." He explained in what way, talking to me as though I were fully grown up and understood the terms he used. It was sad talk, really, even about Timothy—the appendectomy and peritonitis business was being used as an excuse for the fact that never, in a thousand years, in the best of health, could he gain entrance to the school for which he had been entered at birth. And Marie would become more, not less, lame as time passed and her sound leg grew and the affected one did not. Betty's one, most beautiful eye had only been saved temporarily. And so on and so on.

I should have been saddened. Instead I was flattered that he should talk to me so confidentially.

I said, as though to excuse my callousness, "But at least they are happy *now.*"

"Yes. And that is the great thing. To be happy while one can. You should be very happy. Yours was a very simple problem and the end of it is in sight."

With that we came to the top of the rise from which the Clinic was visible.

"You'll be all right now," he said. "I'm going home." He vaguely indicated a direction to the right. "Tomorrow is my free day. Goodnight, Sally. I've talked too much—but a sympathetic listener is a rarity these days."

He walked off, long-legged, free striding along the crest of the ridge. Going downhill I looked back once or twice and once he did too and waved. The distance, the difference in levels or some trick of the light made him seem enormous; I thought of the Colossus of Rhodes; of Atlas bearing the world upon his shoulders.

Back in the Clinic I was rather distressed to find that I had lost the rose which Madame Barthou, coming to the gate with us, had given me. She had asked, "Which is, of all, your favourite, Sally?" and I had said, "That one." It was a deep red velvety rose and she had picked one for me; just perfect, a half-opened bud, smelling of Heaven. I carried it in my hand for a bit and then thought that I must look like those ladies posing for a portrait, so I stuck the long strong stem into the first buttonhole of my blouse and pulled it through the second. A firm anchorage, I thought. But it had worked loose and was lost, and I was grieved.

Dr. Simmons, taking Dr. Martin's place, said, "Very satisfactory." I had lost another pound. "But we must not be abrupt," he said and at lunch I had steak, salad, and egg custard. Thus fortified, I set out to find the slightly longer, but surer road to Madame Barthou's. Walking down in Newtonford I remembered everything that Dr. Martin had told me on the previous evening, all the fundamental hopelessness of the young people whom I had, to be honest, rather envied.

I had never been into Newtonford. The Clinic had its own post box and a kind of shop. I had had no need to go into the village because I was not a cheater, eager to buy biscuits and doughnuts or to drink alcohol at the King's Head. So I was astounded to see that the post office, which was also the general store, stood clamped between the King's Head and a shop that sold antiques. I tried to think back; was it possible that Madame Barthou had said opposite the post office? I crossed over; no road led off from that side either. It was as baffling as the fog; and rather worse because in the fog, lost and cold and frightened as I had been, I had felt well. In myself. Today, suddenly I did not. I felt sick and dizzy and shaky. The custard, I thought . . . too rich for me. I needed to sit down, but not in a house or even a shop where people, meaning kindly, would fuss about and offer me water: so I went into the church porch and sat down on the cold worn stone. I felt better almost immediately and had every intention of going back into the village street and making some inquiries about the elusive road; but then I must have fallen asleep. When I woke up it was past six.

What a wicked waste of an afternoon, I thought, as I trudged back to the Clinic.

In the morning my weight had fallen again, and by this time the change in my bulk was obvious, too; my skirt was quite loose around the waist. Dr. Martin linked his hands together and looked at me approvingly.

"At this rate," he said, "you'll be able to go home. I expect you'll be glad. It's rather a dull way to spend a holiday, isn't it?"

I said, "It *was* until I found Madame Barthou's. Oh, and I want to ask you something, Dr. Martin. The road . . . She said a left turning by the post office in the village, but I couldn't find it. There is in fact no turning off the village street at all."

"Who said there was?"

"Madame Barthou herself. And it was particularly maddening for me not to go yesterday, because after all you told me, I felt I should see them all differently. I'd liked them all, *very much,* from the first but I had rather envied them, too. Living in such a lovely place."

He gave me a look which made me feel instantly that I had done wrong to speak of what he had told me. I remembered medical ethics, strict as the confessional. I said, "Of course I wouldn't breathe a word to anyone else and nothing you said would alter my behaviour towards any one of them. I know only too well what it is to be looked on with pity—there's generally an element of contempt in it."

"How true," he said. He half offered and then withdrew the kind of look he had given me when he said that a sympathetic listener was a rarity. Then he said, "So you couldn't find the road yesterday. How did you get there in the first place?"

I told him about the happy accident that had made an aimless lonely walk project me into such a happy world—happy despite the tragedy it held. I said, "And it grows on you. Have you noticed that? The day when I couldn't get there because of the fog; and yesterday, not finding the road, I was as miserable as sin. I've only been there twice but I feel I belong there, far more than I do at Champton, or anywhere else. Do you feel that? And of course, now that I know that they have *their* problems, I feel I belong even more."

He leafed through the thing which we Clinic patients called our "dossier" as though we were criminals. They were polythene covers with clips and they recorded every physical fact about us: weight, diet, treatment, morning and evening temperatures, everything.

Mine appeared to puzzle him rather. He rustled the papers about and then looked up.

"Sally, have you taken anything that is not mentioned here?"

I thought in terms of diet. "I told you about the fruit, didn't I? And you gave me permission to eat sandwiches at Madame's." Then I remembered; better not mention Mrs. Macer by name. "Oh, I see. Yes, somebody gave me some pills. She said they might work if nothing else did."

"Do you happen to have them with you?"

I handed him the little bottle. He shook a pill out on to his palm and studied it closely.

"How many have you taken?"

"Four. She said one a day."

"The first on Monday?"

"Yes."

"And that was the day when you found Madame Barthou's. Can you work it out yourself and see the connection?" I could, but the answer was almost too appalling to be considered.

"Hallucinations?" I offered the word tremulously, waiting for, longing for a contradiction. But he said, "Exactly. You're obviously very susceptible to this kind of thing."

"You mean I imagined . . . There is no such place. No such people." Just to say it made me feel so utterly bereaved that I could not accept it: I was like people who refuse to believe that a loved one is dead.

"But *you* were there. I didn't imagine *you*, did I?"

He looked away from me for a second, a little uncomfortably, I thought.

"I was part of the fantasy," he said. "That's right, cry if you want to. Don't mind me."

I had not cried over being dropped from the tennis team, over always being tucked away at the back of the school choir, over the ban on being seen in the shop or the thousand and one humiliations obesity had brought upon me. But now I cried and cried. I was not comforted when Dr. Martin explained in his kind, impartial voice that I had been extremely fortunate, both in being discovered in time, and in the *nature* of my hallucinations. Most people, he said, had nightmarish experiences. When he said that, I wished mine had been of that kind. My nightmare was still to come.

All that day the good, sensible half of my brain accepted the situation, and even analysed it with interest; my hallucinations had not imposed themselves upon me, I had ruled them. Because there was so little beauty in my life I had dreamed up roses and fountains. I did not even miss the significance of Madame Barthou's resemblance to my mother; or the fact that I had imposed upon my charming new friends disabilities far worse than my own. Dr. Martin's involvement was all too understandable.

But all the time one half of me was being intelligent and academic, the other half was active too, reminding me that at school some people smoke reefers. . . . They cost four shillings each: but pocket money is one thing I have never been short of. . . .

A Curious Experience

I once had a curious experience; and those who dismiss it as a silly girl's fancy should think again. I was twenty-three at the time and had been married for two years.

When Greg proposed to me, in an offhand way, I said, "You know, or you should do, that I am not the domestic type. If you really want little wifie waiting with a casserole in the oven and your slippers warming by the well-swept hearth, you must look elsewhere."

Greg said that if he had been interested in casseroles and well-warmed slippers, he'd have settled for Amanda. Between me and Amanda, I must confess, it had been as the Duke of Wellington said of Waterloo, "a damned close run thing." But I had won; and for two years Greg and I lived a bit of that happily-ever-after stuff. Happy as larks, as they say, though we had no nest. The firm for which he worked was busy "grooming" him—a nice term for holding the carrot well out of reach at one end and applying stick at the other. Young men with potential must be mobile, must gain experience at all levels, so Greg shuttled about, and I went with him, dragging my portable typewriter, my thick notebook, and a bag of reference books. I had already published one novel, highly praised, savagely criticised, not very profitable.

And then Greg's firm decreed that to complete his grooming, he must spend three months in New York. The wives of the fully groomed are recognised and they may accompany their husbands, expenses paid. But those ungroomed are presumed to be single, foot-loose. I said, "Darling, we simply can't afford it. I'll find some place and tuck in and finish my book. Three months will just about do it." I squinted at him; I do squint when I concentrate. I said, "You go and fall in love with some American floosie and I'll disown you!"

I didn't want him to feel that he must provide for me while we were separated. It had been all right when I tagged about after him—Leeds, Bradford, Glasgow, Edinburgh, Bristol, Norwich. Mostly we had lived in cheap hotels, cheap furnished flats. When we were somewhere where food was provided, we ate what was offered; otherwise I bought things like beefburgers, fish-fingers. Very often my only cooking facility was a frying pan on a gas ring. But I had felt that in a way I earned my keep. For the next three months he would not have even the benefit of my company, and living is expensive in America; so I began to look round for a job. A fairish knowledge of archaeology and ancient history is not the most readily marketable asset and I was quite glad to find part-time employment in a public library in a Suffolk town called Baildon.

There I was also lucky enough to find, not a flat, but a furnished house at an astonishingly low rent—so low indeed that until I saw the place I had the darkest suspicions. The agent made an appointment for me to meet Mrs. Willis at the house, 18 Hillcrest Avenue, on the following afternoon.

Hillcrest Avenue was a quiet cul-de-sac within easy walk of the town centre, at the top of what, in Suffolk, passes for a hill; a very slight rise. It consisted mainly of pairs of semi-detached houses, neither ancient nor modern, all very neat and spruce, with a small garden in front, a longer one behind. The house had a living-room, a dining-room, kitchen, two fair-sized bedrooms and a tiny one, a bathroom. It was completely furnished and good solid stuff.

"Everything," Mrs. Willis said, pulling open a drawer in the kitchen, "down to the last egg spoon." Then, I asked myself, why so cheap? I'd lived in some tatty rooms that called themselves flatlets, and cost double.

She answered my unspoken question.

"I didn't feel justified in asking much because there are so many snags from the tenant's point of view. Insecurity of tenure for one thing. I have to ask for a signed agreement that a week's or at most a fortnight's notice will be accepted. You see, the house belongs to an old aunt of mine. She is very arthritic, quite inca-

pable of looking after herself, and I'm much too far
away. And too busy. Personally I don't think she will
ever leave the Home where she now is. But she is convinced that she will one day find a housekeeper and
be able to come back. It would be unkind to try to
make her see sense. Then she began to fret about the
house standing empty, so I offered to let it and she
quite took to the idea. It's a great nuisance for me. I
have to see potential tenants and generally keep an
eye on things." She glanced around. "It doesn't look
too bad, does it? And you needn't worry about the
garden. A man comes half a day a week."

I felt that this could not be a very profitable enterprise.

"How long has your aunt been in this Home?" I
asked.

Mrs. Willis did mental arithmetic.

"Almost four years," she said. "Fortunately she is
comfortably off. I reckon that she spends at least three
pounds a week, answering advertisements, enclosing
stamped addressed envelopes, most of which never
come back. But there it is, it's her hobby, the one thing
that keeps her alive."

"What about gas and electricity?" I asked.

"Oh, well there I did make a stand. It was such a
nuisance. Having the stuff cut off and put on again and
people going off without paying their bills. So I had
meters. They're under the sink. Well, I must be off. I
hope you'll be happy here. And don't worry too much
about a week's notice. The housekeeper my aunt is
looking for went out with the crinoline."

I moved in later that afternoon, blessing my luck.
I decided that the dining-room, at the back and ad-

joining the kitchen, should be my work- and living-room; one end of the good solid table holding my typewriter and my books, the other my simple haphazard meals. The house had, I now realised, that faintly musty smell that comes from disuse, and I opened all the windows. I had noticed that, despite its nearness to the main shopping centre, this near-suburb had a little shopping precinct of its own. I went down to investigate and found it perfect for my purpose. The general store had a deep freeze and a delicatessen counter. Next door was a laundrette, and beyond it an off-licence and a sub-post-office, both endearingly miniature. A chemist's shop and a hairdresser's completed the semicircle. The housewives in this area were well catered for. And I was one of them. Lucky me. . . .

The rot set in when, the June evening glow waning, I got up and switched on the light. As I type I tend to look up and stare straight ahead, and from the place where I had chosen, what I looked at was a sideboard, of the kind called a chiffonier. Somebody—either the last tenant, or perhaps Mrs. Willis—had given its flat surface a hasty swipe with a duster. The thing was made, I think, of rosewood and the semicircular swipe had left a richly glowing area edged thickly with grey dust. A similar swipe had been made at the delicately framed mirror which formed its back. For some reason that I cannot explain, what remained, dusty on the rosewood, smeary on the glass, bothered me. I simply could not concentrate. I got up, went into the kitchen, found a rather dirty duster, and did a bit of cleaning up. At the same time I took my coffee cup and the plate from which I had eaten my two sausage rolls into the kitchen. Then I sat down, typed a few lines, and knew that "the good spirit" had gone from me.

Who said that cogent thing—the complaint of all writers,

> *What can I do for poesy*
> *Now that the good spirit has gone from me?*
> *What can I do, but useless sit*
> *And over read what I have writ?*

Deadly. The thing we all fear. So check. I wasted an hour in a futile chase and then gave up and went to bed.

In the morning I woke quite early and got out of bed with a thought new to me—I don't want to come back to an unmade bed and a littered kitchen. Up to that morning, although I had never enjoyed absolute squalor, I had been a bit slap happy about time; so long as a bed was made before it was occupied, a cup washed before it was used again, I had been content to shuffle along. What had got into me? I left a neatly made bed, a tidy kitchen behind me when I went to the library. It was Saturday, a busy day, my longest day; ten in the morning to three in the afternoon. At about half-past twelve there was a little lull and I had time to say to the Head Librarian, a pleasant, very academic-looking woman, "Miss Forbes, who wrote that verse beginning, 'What can I do for poesy?' It haunts me and I can't trace it."

She said, "I never heard it. 'Poesy' sounds a bit archaic. Could it be Chaucer?"

Not that it mattered. Just an idle thought. . . .

On my way home I bought enough of what is called "convenience" food to sustain me through the weekend. I'd put in a good session of work. The musty smell inside the house still bothered me and I again opened the windows, this time noticing that they were very dirty. Something impelled me to clean them. . . .

When I told Greg that I was not the domestic type I was being—as I always try to be—flatly truthful. I was born and lived until I was eight in Jamaica, where hired help was plentiful. I was then sent to school in England, and there we made our beds and took turns with the washing-up. After that, college, digs, marriage, and a nomad life. The only ordinary household of which I had ever been a part was that of my grandmother in school holidays, and she not only wanted no help from me, she had the obsessive idea that unless I was studying I was wasting my time—and my parents' hard-earned money. I had never in my life cleaned a window.

From a sour-smelling cupboard under the sink I chose the least filthy of a number of cloths, washed it, and armed with it and a duster and a bucket of water, set to, starting on the dining-room window. I was awkward and slow. As a matter of fact physical activities have never been my thing; hopeless at gym, a mockery on the hockey field. I'm not built for it; too tall, too loosely put together. It took me most of the morning to clean that one window, largely because smears would shift. When I was inside, they were out, and vice versa. I wasted a lot of time making exits and entrances through the kitchen. But in my way I am thorough and shortly before lunch time that window looked a lot better. So much so indeed that I made resolve to clean all the others. In due course; one a day perhaps.

Instant coffee and some fish-fingers restored me and I sat down to type: but the smell of that kitchen cupboard haunted me. I simply could not concentrate. Work done in such circumstances is never good. So I gave in and went to empty and cleanse that offensive retreat. It was a disgusting job, but I was rewarded by finding in the cupboard's farthest corner a container of something called Clearshine, on which the label promised that it took the labour out of window cleaning. Simply spray on and rub. I put this treasure carefully on one side and carried the rest out to the dustbin which was crammed to the brim, largely, it seemed to me, with cartons and packages of discarded foodstuffs, a half-empty pack of biscuits, an unopened pack containing four currant buns, hard as wood, some mouldy green cheese, some evil-smelling fish, still in the can.

I braced myself and remembered that fire purges.

June is not a month when birds suffer much privation, but I gave them the biscuits and the buns, hoping that some woodpecker might come along to deal with the latter. Then I made a bonfire at the farthest end of the back garden. As I returned to the house the sun shone on the clean window and twinkled at me, encouragingly. I needed encouragement. I was bone weary, far too tired now to face the typewriter.

When Mrs. Willis showed me round I had noticed that the sitting-room contained a television set. I'd relax, I thought, as so many thousand do, feet up, in front of the box. But relax I could not. The sofa and the armchairs in this room were covered in a pretty, floral chintz which on closer acquaintance didn't feel or look or even smell right. All through a moderately entertaining programme half my mind was busy with the thought of that laundrette at the foot of the hill and with the thought that tomorrow was Monday, my free day. Few people change books on Mondays; either they have not completed the reading or they are busy with other things. Such as washing at home, or visiting laundrettes. . . .

The thing snowballed. I found out, for instance, that every tenant the house had ever had, had used the same few articles of bed linen, those at the front. Further back there were blankets with which the moths had made merry, and linen that had acquired black stripes simply by being in the cupboard for so long, unused. The laundrette saw a lot of me that week. On my free days, Monday and Thursday, I did a "do-it-yourself" job, on other days I left my bundle on my way to the library, the woman in charge took care of it and I collected it on my way home.

Another ridiculous thing happened, too. In the general store I saw some fresh garden peas. I could just remember how they tasted, cooked with a sprig of mint. I thought—*How silly to buy frozen peas when fresh ones are in season.* . . .

I never studied psychology, but I had read enough to know what was wrong with me. Fundamentally, I thought, I did not like, or was not satisfied with, the story on which I should be working. Second novels are notoriously tricky; anyone can write a first novel . . . I'd lost my nerve; "never glad confident morning again," or I'd chosen a bad subject, or made a wrong approach, or, God help me, I was one of the one-novel gang. And I was taking refuge from my predicament by pretending to be busy with other things. Not a pleasant thought. In fact a thought to flee from. Scrub the kitchen floor; scrub the larder shelves. That activity brought me a bonus; my right wrist gave way and I had to wear a wide leather strap, a kind of miniature buskin, on it for a fortnight. Perhaps professional typists, or those profoundly inspired, can type with one hand. I could not; I could only do little jobs such as separating meat knives from tablespoons in the baize-lined compartments of the kitchen drawer, and bringing order to the things which hung on hooks on the dresser, and throwing out seven—why seven?—stinking old sweaty socks that somebody had secreted in the cupboard under the stairs.

During this period a sweet girl at the library typed four letters to Greg for me and I made shift to sign them, hoping that he would not think that I had taken to drink or drugs. Her spelling was highly individual.

By the time I could discard the strap I knew what was wrong with my book. It was the approach. It was a first-person story and I had been writing in the third. The "good spirit" had not abandoned me; it came back now, very powerful. The character "I" can only relate what he, or she, sees with his own eyes, hears with his own ears. So I needed more than one narrator, and by Heaven I had them, quite suddenly; three of them, three people saying "I" and with their separate, differing stories making a whole. Wonderful! The kind of thing that makes up for the self-distrust, the loneliness, the frustrations . . . I couldn't wait to get started.

I practically ran home, pausing only to buy a slice of veal-and-ham pie, some eggs, a loaf, and a bit of cheese. This was Wednesday—a clear free day tomorrow. Tomorrow, in my immaculate, sweet-smelling house I should sit down, make a fresh start. Prove myself to be not one of the one-book brigade.

But, even as I put my purchases down on the kitchen table, the gas cooker cried out—What about me? Me first!

I had cleaned it once. Like the rest of the house, under a kind of superficial cleanliness, it had been filthy. It was now not filthy, but a little soiled; pulling off a saucepan left-handedly I had spilt some milk.

All right, I said to it, but that is the last thing in the cleaning line that I shall do here. Using my right hand a little cagily, I cleaned it. Then I went into the dining-room, sat down, made the usual sandwich, top paper, carbon, copy paper. With steady confident fingers I typed. Part I. Chapter I. Oh joy! And then the bell rang. I cursed as I went to the door. Somebody collecting, somebody wanting to know if I had put my name on the electoral roll, somebody wanting to know if Mr. A, Mrs. B, Miss C still lived here, and if not was there any forwarding address? Hell, I said; blast. I'll tell whoever it is where to look for a subscription, a vote, a bygone tenant. Squinting I opened the door and there was Mrs. Willis.

She said, "Good evening, Mrs. Fraser. I'm sorry to disturb you so late." In fact it was not late but possibly my squinting scowl made her think that she was not exactly welcome. I said, "Do come in," and she said,

"Well, just for a minute. I am in a bit of a hurry but I was fairly near and I thought I should come and explain . . . personally. A completely unforeseen thing has happened. My aunt has found a housekeeper."

What did she expect me to do? Fall flat on my face? Set myself on fire?

I said, "How nice for her. When do I move?"

We were in the sitting-room with its sparkling window, fresh curtains, crisp, clean chintz. I could see her taking it all in.

"Well," she said, hesitantly. "I *told* her a fortnight. I thought you must have a week's notice and that it would take me at least a week to . . . But you seem to have done it. The place even smells differently. I'm *so* sorry. It does seem a shame."

A thought struck me.

I said, "Would you call your aunt a dominant personality, Mrs. Willis?"

She gave that a second's consideration. "Yes, I would. I mean the way she has stuck to this idea about coming home. Most women of her age . . ."

"And was, I mean *is* she house-proud?"

"Oh, very much so. Terribly particular. She'd empty an ash-tray as soon as you'd ground out the stub. You know?"

"I know," I said; meaning that I knew what had got into me. I'd been for a month possessed.

Mrs. Willis said, "I do hope you don't mind too much. I did want . . ."

"I don't mind a bit," I said truthfully. I thought— Tomorrow the world! A cheap hotel, a bed-sitter, anonymous and undemanding, a chalet in a holiday camp, a caravan, a tent in the middle of a field.

Mrs. Willis touched a chintz cover. She said, "You must have gone to considerable expense. I think it would be only fair to return, shall we say, a week's rent?"

I thought of the wrong story line, with which, in any other surroundings, I might have bashed on; the bad second novel that can ruin one's career. And of the good, sound, wonderful one that was waiting.

I said, "That is very kind, Mrs. Willis. But in fact I owe the house more than it owes me. Living here has been quite an experience. . . ."

A Visit to Claudia

My friend Claudia Gaywood is a woman who, but for her good nature, would be intolerable. I remember her from our earliest school-days when she was a pretty, pampered, rather self-conscious little darling whose possessions and privileges would have been the envy of all if she had not been so willing, indeed so anxious, to share them.

Forty years did little to change her. She retained her looks, her health, and her capacity for facile enthusiasms. She was always adopting—and quickly abandoning—poses, theories, causes. She was one of those people who scan the more serious articles in

Reader's Digest and are at once prepared to discuss
the subjects dealt with as though they had expert quali-
fications. Widowhood eclipsed her for a month or two,
but she emerged, seemingly unscathed, having, I basely
suspected, concentrated upon the correct attitudes and
conventions.

As time went by I met her less and less frequently,
but she was a great letter-writer, an indomitable re-
memberer of Christmases and birthdays; one of those
people who on holidays spend much time buying
highly coloured picture postcards, scribbling "Wish you
were here," and dispatching them to their less fortunate
friends.

Two years ago she went to spend a week-end in
East Anglia with some people named Crawley. She
sent me a postcard from their village, the scrawled
message admonishing me to note that the church had a
Saxon tower. Soon after, I received one of her en-
thusiastic, slightly incoherent letters. The most exciting
thing had happened. The Crawleys had taken her for
a drive and they'd gone through the prettiest village,
with a charming name—Talbot St. Faith; and Claudia
had just said, "Oh, I could live here," and hardly had
she said this than—wasn't it astounding?—there was
the house of her dreams, covered with wisteria, empty
and for sale. So she'd bought it. There was a great
deal of work to be done on it before it was habitable.
If she didn't write for a while, I should understand.

Write, however, she did—copious letters in which
the phrase "I simply must tell you" featured frequently.
A wall was found to be damp and, before it could be
attended to, part of the wisteria had to be cut away.
The cutting had revealed an old lead gutter spout which
bore the date 1720. The room she had decided was to

be the drawing-room had the ugliest little fireplace, impossible to live with, so she'd ordered its removal, and behind it there was a wonderful cavernous brick hearth, for which she must now find a basket grate of the proper period. When it came to stripping off some hideous wallpaper—"magenta roses on a yellow ground, my dear!"—the paper was found to be attached to canvas which had hidden some elegant eighteenth-century pine panelling. When it came to furnishing the place, I gathered that all the antique shops in the region had a boom summer.

Since she was doing precisely what I, given the means, would dearly have loved to do, these letters would have provoked me to envy and malice, but for Claudia's touching desire to share. Before the house was finished, she invited me to go and "rough it" with her. Then, as work progressed, she told me that she was furnishing her guest-room with me in mind, and that on the ground floor there was a darling, snug little room overlooking the garden, very quiet, just the place for me to work in. During her first spring in the house she sent me a large, badly packed box of daffodils and forsythia, with a message: "Since you won't come to Newell's, Newell's must come to you!" She had called the house Newell's after a former owner, about whom, she said, she would tell me when we met; it was too long a story to put into a letter.

A number of circumstances prevented me from taking advantage of these warm invitations, and Claudia had owned Newell's for more than two years when I found myself faced with temporary homelessness. It was then November, not everyone's choice for a month in the country, but I like the contrast between miry ways and glowing firesides, and I like the pattern of

bare boughs against the sky. Also I had heard a good
deal about Claudia's central heating. So I wrote, and
within an hour of receiving my letter she was telephon-
ing me; my visit was the one thing to which she, and
Newell's, had been looking forward.

I arrived while there was still light enough to see by.
The house had the flat front, the evenly spaced windows, the parapet, the wide fan-lighted door of the
Georgian heyday; but behind the parapet, rearing
against the November sky, was a cluster of chimneys,
some twisted, some of moulded brick. I thought, with
a pang of unworthy pleasure, that I could tell Claudia
that a date on a gutter spout was not infallible evidence
of a house's age. And then, there she was, pretty as
ever, ebullient, warmly welcoming.

She showed me where to put my car and insisted
upon carrying in the heavier of my two suitcases. She
said that she was glad to see that I had brought my
typewriter; she hoped I'd stay for months and months.
I looked pale, she thought, and tired. Country life and
air would do me a world of good. So would the atmosphere of Newell's, so eighteenth-century—I should soak
it in and be inspired. Wouldn't it be thrilling if I
settled here long enough to write a book!

In the attractive hall, she deposited my case at the
foot of the staircase and then opened a panelled door
into a cloakroom. "If you want to wash," she said, "then
we'll have tea right away and I'll show you your room
later on."

Her drawing-room was beautiful; it was also warm
and full of the pleasant, earthy scent of chrysanthemums. The basket grate was heaped with logs and

the firelight flickered on well-polished surfaces, on china and silver.

Claudia had, as I feared, made the eighteenth century her own. The silver tray and the tea service were Georgian, and she made the tea at table, ladling the tea from a genuine old caddy with a genuine old caddy spoon, and pouring water from a spirit kettle. We ate tiny savoury sandwiches. "They're made with Gentleman's Relish," she said. "I'm not quite sure that it was known in Captain Newell's day, but I somehow feel that he would have approved of it." Some streak of perversity made it impossible for me to ask the obvious question, "And who was Captain Newell?" There were saffron buns and caraway cake.

Claudia said, "I found the most wonderful cookery book. The *Olde English Cook Book*—full of original recipes. They're marvellous, though a bit lavish with cream and butter. I shall get fat if I'm not careful!"

At seventeen she had weighed eight and a half stones, at thirty she had weighed eight and a half stones, and judging by the look of her, she weighed about that now. She recognised this as one of her blessings, and was inclined to draw attention to the fact, either directly or indirectly. This did not endear her to her contemporaries who, at forty, tended to grow too plump or too lean.

For the next hour she regaled me with detailed accounts of where she had discovered every article of furniture, every ornament in the room, the state it had been in when discovered and the price she had paid for it. She did this, not boastfully, but gloatingly, as well she might; she'd acquired some marvellous bargains.

"And I never minded buying things earlier than the eighteenth century," she said earnestly. "It stands to reason, doesn't it, that people came here bringing their treasures and heirlooms. And of course I was sensible over mattresses and chairs and kitchen gadgets. After all, think of the help people had in those days; we need some compensation."

Not that she was without help. She had wonderful help, a woman named Mrs. Hawk who came from the village every day on a bicycle. She was actually coming back this evening to dish up the dinner and clear up afterwards.

"There again I'm singularly lucky. Most people can't get any help in the evenings, or if they do, their women are clumsy and smash things. Mrs. Hawk was a parlourmaid before she married, and she treats all my things as though they were her own. Len and Helen Crawley are coming to dinner. You'll like them and they're very anxious to meet you. It'll be nice for me to introduce them to somebody; they've introduced me to some charming people. You know, a lot of people complain that as they grow older they have fewer friends; honestly, I have more."

It was true; but it sounded smug.

Presently she began to move about, getting ready for the pre-dinner drinks.

"I always have Madeira nowadays; it is so in keeping. But of course I have martinis and sherry as well. Whisky too." She kept her liquor in a cabinet which she explained to me was Chinese Chippendale; and the olives and nuts were in sweetmeat dishes.

By that time I was a little edgy, a little less fond of the eighteenth century than I had been. Then she put her arm around me, and she was soft and warm and sweet-smelling, "Now we'll go up. I'm simply longing to show you your room."

At the foot of the stairs we had a brief wrangle over who should carry the larger case; this time I won. Claudia took the small one and went tipping ahead of me. The staircase, like the chimneys, considerably predated the house front. The steps were shallow and sloped slightly from left to right; the banister posts were intricately carved, the handrail very thick. I noticed all this as I mounted the first few stairs, and then all I was aware of was an increasing difficulty in moving upward. The distance between me and Claudia increased, and as it did I moved more slowly, with more effort. The case dragged me backwards. I realised that I was badly out of condition. I'd been living on a fifth floor and using the lift. I led a sedentary life, was unused to carrying heavy objects.

Claudia dumped what she was carrying and sped down again. "I told you you should have let me carry that. I'm a lot stronger than I look." She stood beside me on the wide stair and attempted to take the suitcase. Infuriated by this sidelong reference to her Dresden-china, please-take-care-of-me appearance which is in such strong contrast to my own, I wouldn't let go, so we went up the stairs with the case between us. And she was strong, I admit.

There was a landing, with some doors and an archway, which wasn't even Tudor—late thirteenth or early fourteenth century I'd have said, if asked. Beyond was a short passage and a door. Claudia threw it open, switched on a light, and said, "There!" in a voice of triumph.

It was quite the prettiest room I'd ever slept in. The

panelled walls were painted a muted bluish-green, the carpet matched exactly. There was a four-poster, smaller than a double, wider than a single bed, curtained, covered, and valanced with glazed chintz, white, scattered all over with moss rose buds. The dressing-table was a Queen Anne chest with a swing mirror and silver candlesticks made into electric lamps.

"It's lovely," I said with genuine feeling.

"You haven't seen half." She opened what looked like a section of panelling. "This was a powder-closet, it's your bathroom. And this"—she opened another section—"is a clothes-closet. I had the rail put in. There were hooks. How did they manage, just with hooks? All those voluminous clothes!" Her voice changed. "Well, I'm glad you like it. As I told you, I had you in mind all the time."

She gave me a fond smile and flitted away.

I am inclined to view with caution any statement attributing human qualities to inanimate things: and I had just been surfeited with accounts of how this house felt towards Claudia and how pieces of furniture had just stood there simply crying out to her to buy them. So I hesitated before admitting, even to myself, that the pretty room, appointed with me in mind, showed me an unwelcoming face. Instead I thought that it was an exceptionally cold room. The green was the green of deep cool water, the chintz had a glacial look. There was a radiator between the windows and it occurred to me that Claudia had forgotten to turn it on. I went over to it and was surprised to find it scaldingly hot. It failed to warm the room however, and it took a definite effort of will to remove my jacket and jersey and don a thin dress.

Suddenly I felt miserable. I was certain that Claudia —for all her sweetness of manner—didn't really want *me;* she wanted an appreciative eye, a listening ear. I thought of alternative arrangements I might have made for housing myself during my homeless interim; then, in a burst of most unusual self-pity, I wondered whether anyone, anywhere, wanted me, or ever had.

Almost in a panic I fled down to the drawing-room and the fire; and once I was there my mood changed. The Crawleys arrived and proved themselves excellent company; two martinis dispelled my ersatz woes. The dinner, cooked, as Claudia was bound to inform us, according to the *Olde English Cook Book,* was first-class and beautifully served. It was not until half-past eleven, when the Crawleys announced, reluctantly, that they must go, that I remembered that I, too, must go—to bed—to sleep in that frigid, unfriendly room.

Claudia went to the door with her guests and I began to empty ash-trays and plump up cushions. When she came back she sat on a low stool, lighted a cigarette, and began to talk about the Crawleys, and then about mutual friends in the past.

Suddenly, from somewhere undefined, there came a dull, heavy thump. I gave a start, recovered myself, remembered Mrs. Hawk, and said, "Your woman stays late."

"Oh, she's been gone ages," Claudia said. "I see what you mean. Ten o'clock *is* late for country people."

She seemed not to have heard the thud and I was on the point of mentioning it when I remembered reading an account of a house generally reckoned to be haunted. One of the manifestations was a dull thumping, heard by some people and not by others. And of course, as soon as I had entertained that cheerful thought, another thud sounded. Cold spots were physically significant, too.

Claudia said, "Poor Ennie, I am a brute keeping you up. You look quite pale. How about a nightcap and then straight into bed?"

I accepted the nightcap with, maybe, overmuch avidity.

This time, going upstairs, though I carried nothing but a handbag, I had even more difficulty in mounting. I felt as though something soft, yet unyielding, was barring the way. I fought my way up, thinking how ridiculous the whole thing was, but made little progress until Claudia, coming behind me, put her hands on my waist and said, "You hardly know how to put one foot in front of the other. I shall bring you your breakfast in bed."

I undressed quickly and climbed into bed, glad to find that it held an electric blanket which had been switched on by Mrs. Hawk. The sheets were of fine linen, the pillows of down, the mattress springy, the covers almost weightless. A very comfortable bed, I thought, and composed myself for sleep. But sleep was far away. I lay there and suffered again in retrospect every slight, every snub, every injustice I had ever experienced in my life. When I reached the point where my mother preferred my brother to me—as what natural mother wouldn't?—I got up angrily and swallowed one of the sleeping pills which I carry, "just in case," and seldom need. After a time I did sleep, but I was soon awake again, practically certain that another of those thumps had awakened me. I lay waiting for another, which did not come. What did come was the memory of every ghastly, dreadful thing I'd ever heard of: murder, atrocities of every kind reeled out pictorially before my mind's cringing eye. Then my joints began to ache and I thought of the medieval torture thing known as Little Ease, a cage in which the prisoner could neither sit nor stand nor lie, and every joint became inflamed, and he lived for months in agony. I swallowed another pill and slept at last, to wake with a dry mouth and aching head to find Claudia by the bedside, gay and fresh as a daisy, holding a tray.

She asked how I had slept, and I muttered, "Not very well." One often didn't one's first night in a strange bed, she said; besides, she could see that I was overtired. She drew back the curtains and said that it was a lovely morning for the time of year, a slight mist, with the sun just breaking through. How would I like to go for a drive to Lavenham, a famous old wool town, with a wonderful church and an inn where we could lunch? She'd drive; I need do nothing but sit back and enjoy the scenery.

Before I went downstairs I wrote a letter to a friend in High Wycombe begging her to telephone me and demand that I go there immediately. I stamped the letter but did not put it into my handbag. I intended to slip it into the pocket of my overcoat whence I could withdraw it as soon as I sighted a post box. Why I should act so furtively I don't know. Guests are allowed to write letters. But the ruse savoured of ingratitude, and I did feel guilty.

I went down. Claudia was ready. Mrs. Hawk was

humming a hymn in the kitchen. I remembered my letter.

"I've forgotten something," I said.

"I'll get the car out," Claudia said. "Isn't this a lovely morning for November? Aren't we lucky?"

I turned to mount the stairs, struggled against whatever it was, made no headway, came out in goosepimples, and gave up.

All that I saw that day, the charming, unspoiled countryside, the medieval town, the fine church, the low dark bar and the raftered dining-room of the inn, I saw through a veil of grey muslin. I was astonished at myself, having always thought that I was a fairly down-to-earth person; I was frightened; above all I wanted to talk about the thing. If I could only say to somebody, "There's something on the stairs and in the guest-room at Newell's that isn't quite canny," I should have felt better; just as people feel better as soon as they can describe the symptoms that they fear indicate some dread disease. But the last person to whom I could say that was Claudia, who'd lived there so happily all alone, who had no suspicion.

Over the lunch, which I could make only a pretence of eating, she said, "Now we'll go home by Long Melford. The church there is even better. And that way back I can show you the house Len and Helen wanted me to have. They were terribly *against* Newell's. They thought it was much too run down, and too isolated. They thought I'd be lonely." She gave a little laugh and her face took on an expression that I remembered so well, the lucky-girl-with-yet-another-present-to-display. "I daresay you'll think this is all whimsy-whamsy, but I never am alone in that house; I never have been. You see, I have a ghost."

Following upon the thoughts I had been thinking, this was a shock; but something warned me that what she was talking about and what I was thinking about were two very different things.

"Surely you don't *mind,* Ennie. I wouldn't have mentioned it, not for worlds, if I thought you'd mind. I thought you'd be intrigued. And honestly, there's no need to mind. He's a most friendly ghost, my Captain Newell."

I said, "Oh yes, you promised to tell me. . . ."

She said, "I've always thought I was a teeny bit psychic. It was very odd. I went into that house when it had been empty and neglected for twenty years, all dust and dry rot and cobwebs. But it welcomed me, it really did. Then, when I came to look at the record of title, one name—Jeremiah Newell—just leaped out at me. And I realised that he'd loved the house; he lived there for thirty-two years, longer than anybody else, from 1799 to 1831. An old sailor, home from the sea. With a sea-chest, perhaps, and a parrot. He loved that house and he knows I love it. So he is my friend."

I said, "How do you know? Have you seen or heard . . . anything?"

"Oh no. I just feel it. You can't ask for evidence about a thing like that. You just . . . well, you sort of tune in. I think he'd had an unhappy love affair and never married. . . ."

"Did you ever try to find out anything about him?" She shook her head. "I felt that would spoil it somehow. I think of him as tall and thickset, sunburned and weatherbeaten—and smoking a clay pipe.

After all, it isn't what you know in such a case, it's what you *feel*."

I persisted. "And what *do* you feel, exactly?"

"I told you. A warm, friendly atmosphere; a sense of approval, and of protection."

"Against what?"

"Oh, whatever it is that women living alone dread. Feeling lonely, or burglars. I just feel that nothing could happen to me with Captain Newell around. That's why I named the house for him. It's *his* still, we share it. Mind you, Ennie, I wouldn't say this to just anybody. I never mentioned it to Len and Helen. They were so sweet. They thought I ought to have a dog for company, so they gave me one of their boxer's pups. She was a dear and I loved her, but she was absolutely hysterical."

I said cautiously, "Can dogs be that?"

"She was—or the canine equivalent. She had a thing about the stairs. She would never come up them, no matter how I enticed her; and she'd stand in the hall with her hackles up and howl. You never heard anything so eerie. In the end it got me down and I had to ask Len to take her back."

I know now why people in perilous situations make such bad, macabre jokes. I said, "Maybe she was aware of Captain Newell."

Claudia laughed gaily. "What an idea! I'm sure he loved dogs and they loved him. Mind you, I don't deny that some dogs are credited with ESP; but if she'd had it, she'd have jumped and wagged her bit of tail. She was a victim of this overbreeding, poor dear. You know, Ennie, you're more in need of a break than you realised. You've hardly eaten anything and you're looking terribly pale. I think we'll leave Long Melford for another day and go straight home."

Back at the house I made the discovery that whatever it was that was opposed to my mounting the stairs allowed Claudia free passage, and that if I let her go first she seemed to carry me along in her airway, so to speak. But my room still regarded me with a cold, inimical eye.

My letter had gone from the dressing-table and when I mentioned it, Claudia said not to worry; she was sure Mrs. Hawk had taken it to post. "I'm a bit careless about such things myself, and she's very conscientious."

I asked Claudia if I might have a look at all her records pertaining to the house, and she produced them willingly. "I couldn't bother with them," she said, "so badly written and all those *whereas*es and *the aforesaid*s."

The earliest was dated 1720, which, in conjunction with the gutter spout, had deluded Claudia; but it was a record of transfer between William Martin and Thomas Pratt. Thomas Pratt had sold the property some six years later to Susannah Cobb, widow, whose occupancy was brief—only seven months. In fact, the place had changed hands with a frequency that was remarkable. Jeremiah Newell, sea captain, whose beautiful calligraphy would have distinguished him anywhere, was the only person who had stayed there any length of time. But Walter George Isell, from whom Claudia Maybrook, widow, had purchased the property, ran Jeremiah pretty close; he'd owned it for twenty years. I remarked upon this and Claudia said, "Oh yes; but he never *lived* here. He lived up at the Park and he bought it for his agent. Now that is a very sad story and it accounts for the house standing empty so long. Not of course that I can be sorry, because in my heart I must confess that I'm glad the house waited for me."

"What happened?"

"Well, Mrs. . . . I'm sorry the name escapes me, Mrs. Agent was going to have a baby, so they needed more room. So Mr. Isell bought this place and Mrs. Agent came over to measure for curtains or something. You know how our generation was—take no notice, don't let nature dictate, carry on regardless. She probably shouldn't have been exerting herself at all. She came here alone and had a fall. It brought on a frightful miscarriage and she died. So then the house just stood and rotted, because the agent, naturally, didn't need any more room, and wouldn't have wanted to live here anyway. Quite understandable."

"Did she fall on the stairs?"

Claudia gave me a sharp look. "As a matter of fact, yes. How did you guess? You know, it's funny, I've always felt that if *you* came here, you'd sense . . . you know," she waved a pretty hand, "all the stored-up history. Young Mrs. Isell told me about the tragedy at a cocktail party. I think she was trying to explain why the house was in such a state. Nobody seemed to realise that I loved saving it."

That night was worse than the one before. Determined to have no nonsense, firmly expecting that on the morrow I should be safe in High Wycombe, I took two pills and fell asleep almost immediately. I woke to find myself rigid with cold, though the bedclothes were undisturbed. I switched on the blanket and it grew warm; so did such parts of my body as were in contact with it; the rest of me stayed cold. Perhaps it was that that made me begin to think about my death, the form it would take, where, when.

It was supremely idiotic. I knew that everybody must die, that every birth certificate was a death warrant. So far as I knew I was in perfect health; I was forty-six years old and women are long-lived creatures. There was plenty of time to prepare for death. But I thought about dying, about the possibility of being buried alive. My heart fluttered, my breathing became difficult, I had horrible cramps. I tried to read, but the print danced. I was forced to consider my most urgent fear—the fear of going blind.

There I capitulated. I got out of bed, put on my slippers and dressing-gown, snatched up my book, and retreated. As I went through the arch to the landing, I heard one of the thuds.

In the drawing-room a last log smouldered dimly; I turned it over and added more fuel. I poured myself a drink, smoked a cigarette, read for a little, felt naturally sleepy, arranged myself on the sofa, and slept.

Claudia woke me, anxious, clucking, inquisitive. I told her that I suffered from insomnia, that I had come down for a drink, felt sleepy suddenly, and snatched the chance of a snooze. She has very clear blue eyes and in them I could see *Insomniac?* change to *Dipsomaniac* as plainly as the signs change at Piccadilly Circus. But she said she'd always thought that the life I lead must be a terrible strain and now she knew. What I needed was rest and quiet and looking after. All these she was ready to provide, starting now with breakfast.

I imagined my letter arriving at High Wycombe and managed breakfast quite well.

It was another mild, windless, silver-gilt day, and presently Claudia suggested that we should drive out to Clare Priory. A fascinating place, she said, built in 1248, dissolved in 1538, used as a private house until 1953 when the Augustinian friars had bought it back and made it into a religious house again. I was just about to concoct some excuse for staying in the house for an hour when Mrs. Hawk arrived. Claudia asked about my letter and the woman said she hadn't seen it; had she seen it, she would certainly have posted it. Claudia said that I must have had it in my bag after all and I pretended to agree. There would be no reprieve from High Wycombe, I thought, with an inward tremor, so I might as well go to Clare.

It is there for all to see and the friars welcome visitors, so there is no need to describe it. Not that I could; I was too much concerned by my own situation to give attention to anything. Perhaps this is why I was stupid enough when a sudden turn brought us to the foot of a staircase, to move towards it. The young friar who was showing us round stepped forward very quickly and lifted his arm, barring my way. He smiled. "No. I am sorry. Ladies are not allowed." He indicated a notice, in Latin, on the wall.

Claudia said brightly, "Of course. Dormitories." Then she looked at me and exclaimed, "Oh, Ennie! We've tired you out again. You look so pale. Are you all right?"

I couldn't speak. It would be wrong to say that the truth had flashed upon me, for in cases like this who can decide what *is* the truth? I only know that the arm out-thrust to bar my way here was so directly related with what I had felt on the staircase at Newell's that I was overcome by an appalling understanding. I daresay I had turned pale.

They took me back into the parlour with its massive carved beams, set me in a chair, and fussed round—at least Claudia fussed; the friar fetched a glass of ice-cold water, which I sipped, wishing it had been something hot and strong. As soon as I could speak I said, "I'm all right now. Sorry to be such a nuisance." Then I asked what seemed to me to be a vital question.

"Did this priory have subsidiary houses in the vicinity?"

The question—certainly the most intelligent one he had heard from me that morning—seemed to please the friar.

"Indeed yes, several. They were minor establishments, for rest, or for correction." He smiled, just as noticeably abstemious people smile when they talk about last night's binge. "There are bad friars sometimes, you know." Then, grave again, he added, "Often the names remain. Friars' Place, Priory Farm, and so on."

"My house could have been one of them," Claudia said, all excitement. "It was called Priory Farm at one time." She had read her record of title more closely than she had admitted. "But when I bought it, it was called Pratt's, just Pratt's. Such a snatchy-sounding word. So I changed it again."

"Back to the original?" the friar asked.

"I'm afraid not. I named my house for a friend, a very dear old friend."

She threw me a knowing look.

I felt a little sick. Thinking herself psychic, and all the time so oblivious, so immune. Wire a chest of drawers to a television aerial, I thought, and what do you get? I thought of Susannah Cobb who had fled after seven months; and of the agent's wife, doubly unwelcome because of her pregnancy. I thought of me. All my thoughts led to the same decision: I did not intend to spend another night in that house.

I had an excuse ready. As soon as Claudia and I were alone together, I should tell her that my tired spells, my pallor, were the result of renewed trouble with my slipped disc; I should say that it was absolutely essential that I get to London while I could still drive. I must see my osteopath.

About leaving her alone, I had no compunction. She'd lived in the house for two years and felt nothing of its real atmosphere; she could live there to her life's end and babble about her friendly ghost. There leaped into my mind the memory of something from school-days: Gresham's law, which says that at any time, in any place, bad currency will oust the good. And in Captain Jeremiah Newell, his clay pipe, his parrot, and his sea-chest, Claudia had bad psychic currency enough and to spare.

"And now, if you are feeling better," the friar said, "I would like to show you our chapel. We are particularly proud of the restoration work in our chapel."

Mindful of the plan I proposed, I murmured that I wouldn't walk any more, I'd sit here and wait.

"Poor Ennie. What a shame. Would you like to go straight home?"

"No, no. You see the chapel and anything else you want to. I'm all right here."

"I would like just a peep. If you're sure . . ." She went off, tripping and chirping. The friar opened a door and I saw an enclosure with flower beds and trees and grey paving.

After a minute or two I heard a distant cry which could just have been one of exaggerated admiration from Claudia, but which sounded rather more like one of pain. It was the latter, I realised, when the door opened again and revealed Claudia, leaning heavily upon the arm of the friar, who looked very much concerned. She was favouring her left ankle, which was already swelling.

The pupils in her blue eyes were wide; where her face was unrouged, it looked chalky. She was positively being very brave.

"Don't say it," she said, with a ghastly attempt at sprightliness. "These ridiculous heels! I know. I know." Then she swayed and we had to put her in the chair and force her head down. Fortunately I had not drunk all the water.

She soon recovered and was full of apologies, to the friar and to me.

"Darling, I'm so sorry. I'm afraid you'll have to drive home."

"If I may suggest, to the hospital," the friar said. "It is a severe wrench, you may have broken a bone. It would be advisable to have an X-ray."

Looking down at the bulge above the edge of Claudia's high-heeled, low-cut court shoe, I could but agree.

By the time the X-ray had been taken and had revealed that no bones were broken, and we had found our way to Casualty and Claudia's ankle had been firmly strapped, and we'd made a donation to the Friends of the Hospital, and she had hobbled back to the car, and I had driven home, the afternoon light was failing. Afternoons are short in November.

"I really am the most lucky girl," Claudia said, "to have this happen while you are with me. It'll be dull for you, darling, for a day or two, but we'll make up for it after."

My own luck didn't bear thinking about. At least another couple of nights here. Even had my slipped disc been genuine, I couldn't have left her in this extremity.

I made one futile effort at self-protection. I suggested that the stairs would be too much for her and that she should stay on the drawing-room sofa. I reckoned, rather wildly, that I could force myself upstairs *once,* now, before it was fully dark, and throw down unbreakable things, carry down the rest, all that we could possibly need for the night. Then I could say that I didn't like to leave her, and sleep in a chair or on the hearth rug.

But no, oh no. Claudia would have none of that. She was being brave. She could get upstairs all right. I mustn't worry. She'd go to bed and, if I would be kind enough, I could bring her a tray. The meal was all ready, Mrs. Hawk had seen to it. All I had to do was put a few things on a tray; then I could read or write or watch television. She was so sorry to be such a nuisance.

We went upstairs easily enough, side by side, one step at a time, Claudia holding on to me with her left hand and leaning on the banister rail with the other. In her bedroom I switched on her blanket and folded back the covers and waited, while she, hopping and leaning on this piece of furniture and that, donned an extraordinarily seductive nightdress and did a lot of complicated things to her face and hair.

Finally installed in bed and looking like herself again, a full-blown, sweetly scented pink rose, she said, triumphantly, "There darling, I'm all right now. And you know, I've just remembered, you've had no lunch. I am so sorry! Just slap a snack on a tray for me, and then have a lovely long evening to yourself."

I had a strong desire to break down and cry, to say that I wanted to stay here in this warm, rosy-lighted room, in the safe company of the blind, deaf, *lucky* woman whose only ghost was the trite, conventional product of her own imagination. But if I did that, I should have to say why. . . .

I went down; the kitchen was reassuring; the refrigerator purred like a contented cat. The soup was in a saucepan, needing only to be heated; the bowls were ready. I took a large tray and tried to concentrate upon gathering together everything two people could need for a simple meal. But my mind was distracted: part of it remembered the friar's out-thrust arm, the Latin words on the wall, the little quip about bad friars; another part was wondering how long Claudia would be incapacitated—how many other evenings should I be in this situation?

While the soup heated, I looked to the fastenings of the door, no cheerful task, since I was locking myself in with what I dreaded. All the time I was moving nearer to the moment when I must face, alone, what waited for me on the stairs. I poured the soup, put the lids on the bowls, lifted the tray, and went into the hall. I was quivering a little and cringing already.

Outside the drawing-room door I paused. A drink might help. Also Claudia might be expecting some of her precious Madeira. *Excuses!* my mind shouted at me; *you're just putting off the bad minute.* I set the tray on a low table and went to the cabinet. There I slopped a generous measure of gin into a glass, added a drop of vermouth, and gulped it down, tasting nothing. It ran searingly into my empty stomach and seemed to take fire there. Warmed and heartened and with steadier hands, I poured a glass of Madeira and another, more normally proportioned, martini, and found room for two glasses on the tray.

As I moved towards the door, I heard one of those dull thuds. Familiar now with the layout of the house, I knew where it came from. My own room, immediately overhead. It sounded like a warning—*I'm waiting!*

Unnerved by this, but pot-valiant, I advanced towards the stairs.

At the fourth step I met opposition so strong that I recoiled and almost fell backwards; I just managed to retain my balance and to stand there teetering. I thought of Claudia, waiting in her pink room, and knew that with her I should be safe. *Sanctuary, I must reach it.* But I might as well have tried to walk through a wall. I was so much aware of personal animosity, a direct threat, that I addressed an appeal to whatever it was. *I understand,* I said in my mind, *you were one of those who found their vows of chastity hard to keep;*

some woman was a temptation to you, so you hate us all; but I'm harmless, I assure you.

Then I realised what I was doing and thought—*I'm going mad*. I was shaking so violently that all the things on the tray jangled together; soup, Madeira, martini slopped on to the tray and spilled over, tepid on my icy hands.

I thought—*I'll call Claudia; she for some reason is immune. She'll come.* I called, I screamed her name, but it was like it is sometimes in a nightmare. There was no sound. In a nightmare, at that point, one wakes. But I was awake, still senselessly throwing myself against that invisible barrier.

Then, and it was horrible, I thought that I could smell my opponent; a blend of boiled mutton, human sweat, and stale incense.

I began to pray. "God help me. Please God help me." I started on the Lord's Prayer, one splinter of my shattered mind registering surprise at how glibly the words came. I reached "And deliver us from evil . . ." and stuck there, like a Gramophone needle. "Deliver us from evil, from evil, from evil, evil, evil. . . ." But I was not delivered.

Incoherent, on the verge of madness, I remembered Captain Newell and the immunity with which Claudia passed up these stairs. *You may not like me very much,* I cried in my mind, *but I'm trying to take this to your friend.*

Almost instantly—and crazy as this may sound, it is true—the unpleasant mutton-sweat-and-incense odour was replaced by the smell of a very strong tobacco; and the pressure against me withdrew so suddenly that I, leaning against it, fell forward. If I had had a free hand with which to clutch at the banister, I could have saved myself, even then. As it was, I fell, spiralling down into darkness, to the accompaniment of the noise that a laden tray makes when it falls downstairs.

The next thing I knew was a feeling of warmth and comfort, a sensation of being cherished that I had not known since childhood. I lay and savoured this for a while. Then I looked about me and realised that I was in Claudia's room, in her bed. The rose-shaded lamp made an island of light; and her sweet, floral scent enveloped me. *Safe,* I thought, *saved.* I lay and enjoyed that feeling which is one that most people in civilised countries seldom know.

Presently I was aware of voices—Claudia's, and a deep, male one, with a burr to it.

She said, "No harm done. I just hopped."

He said, "But it couldn't have happened at a more unfortunate time. Would you know, is it a frequent occurrence?"

She said, "I couldn't say. You see, it's some years . . . But I think I should have heard. Anyway, one mustn't judge, must one? I mean . . . People like her live on their nerves, and it is recognised now that alcohol does relieve tension. And she hasn't had a happy life, poor girl."

Talking about me?

"Well, Mrs. Gaywood, I can assure you there's no injury. I doubt if she'll develop bruises. They fall lightly. And there's nothing for you to worry about. Let her lie and sleep it off."

They *were* talking about me; and in what terms! Not that it was surprising, what with the neat gin I'd gulped, and the Madeira and martini from the tray. I must reek like a distillery, I thought; but still . . .

I roused myself and said about the most damning thing I could, in the circumstances.

"I'm not drunk!" I said, in a loud, belligerent voice.

Claudia limped towards the bed; she wore a negligee that matched the nightdress.

"Darling!! Nobody even thought that you were."

"He did! Oh yes he did, I heard him." I lifted myself and looked towards the dark bulk with the stern, unmistakably Scottish, unmistakably doctory, face.

"This is Dr. MacGraw," Claudia said. "He helped me carry you up. You're in my bed because that was warm and yours wasn't. You fell, Ennie. It's all my fault, making you hump that great heavy tray. But you aren't hurt, only shaken a bit, and run-down. And I'm going to take the greatest care of you."

"You're sweet," I said. "That's what you are, *sweet!* Everybody loves you and no wonder." To my profound astonishment I found that I was crying. "You don't know what it's like for the rest of us." I gulped. "Even at school you were Miss Fraser's pet. You never lost a friend, you never gained a pound. You've lived here for two years and nothing touched you. I've been here two days and look at me! I can't think why we don't hate you, you're so lucky. If you went into hell, you'd come out with a bunch of snowdrops."

Claudia said helplessly, "Oh Ennie!"

Dr. MacGraw said, "A sedative would be the thing, but I don't like mixing with all that alcohol."

"What do you mean! All that alcohol! One miserable drink. Taken as medicine, that's what it was." I sobbed harder. "I've had a terrible experience—but nobody is sorry for me!" Some remaining crumb of sense in my mind warned me not to go on about my experience. It also took notice of the threat implicit in Claudia's promise to look after me. *Oh God,* I thought, *she'll try to make me stay in bed in that room through the archway.* I made an effort to control myself, to be crafty again. "A terrible experience," I repeated. "I happen to suffer from a slipped disc which causes me exquisite agony. I faint with pain. Frequently. As a matter of fact, if Mrs. Gaywood hadn't sprained her ankle, I intended to go to London this very afternoon and put myself in the hands of my osteopath."

Dr. MacGraw stepped forward a little and regarded me more coldly than a doctor should regard even a dipsomaniac—and after all he must have seen *real* drunks in his life—and said, "If you have faith in your osteopath, I should advise you to consult him without delay. For one thing, Mrs. Gaywood is in no condition to look after you just now."

"Oh thank you," I said. "Thank you for the passport."

They both looked at me blankly; then Dr. Mac-Graw put his hand on Claudia's sleeve and drew her away. I heard him say the effects take time to wear off. I thought, *how true.* I doubted if they ever would, completely, or that I should ever be quite the same again.

The Watchers

She looked up at the rather ugly house as though seeing it for the first time, hesitated for a second, and put the key in the door. As she did so the street lamp flashed on and everything outside its radiance grew darker. Behind the open door the hall was a black cavern. Before entering she reached in and pressed a switch.

It looked exactly as she had left it; ordinary enough, indeed pretty. To her left, on an oak chest the big blue and white bowl held a few late pink dahlias and some sprays of Michaelmas daisies. On her left the handsome grandfather clock stood mute. Underfoot, almost covering the stone floor, was a Persian runner, old, a little faded, but still colourful.

She hurried into the kitchen, a warm, gay place on which they had spent rather more than they could afford. "You'll spend a lot of time there," Hal had said. "And the best is cheapest in the long run." The splendid new boiler, the stainless-steel sink unit, the rose-patterned Formica surfaces, and the strip lighting mocked her. The long run! Eight months; then the sudden, unexpected promotion that look Hal to Wisborough, seventy miles away.

The window over the sink looked directly into the garden and the night stared in. Not looking at the black oblong—once she had seen her own reflection and gone rigid with shock—she drew the curtains hastily. Had she known that the bus route had been changed and her return would be delayed, she would have drawn every curtain before leaving the house to make such meagre purchases as were necessary to a woman on her own.

With the curtains drawn the kitchen seemed safe and cosy; she would have liked to stay there and make a cup of tea, but she knew that she could not settle until she had made her round and seen that all was well. And before she could face that she must have a tiger-frightener. She made a little grimace as she thought how lightly people used that term; people who did not know what fear was. There was only about an inch of gin left in the bottle; she made a mental note about replacing it. Bottle neck and glass chattered, though she was very careful, having broken several things lately. She took the gin neat, shuddering at the first gulp; she normally drank, if anything, sweet brown sherry. Nine days of living under threat had taught her that gin was more effective. Waiting for it to hearten her she distributed her purchases; to all intents and purposes an ordinary woman in a better-than-average kitchen; but she moved almost noiselessly, alert and wary, listening, like someone in a primaeval jungle.

She went into the hall and unlocked the door of the dining-room. It was not much used, since there was room to eat in the kitchen and they had seldom entertained; there had been so little time, what with the moving in and the alterations, to make friends. Lack of friends was, indeed, one of her troubles at this moment; in all Ashforth there was nobody whom she could ring up and say, "Come round, I'm feeling . . . lonely." She put that thought away and looked around the dining-room, first with apprehension; then with approval. It looked occupied, with the little posy in the centre of the table, and though it was fundamentally an ugly room, the solid Victorian mahogany furniture which had been her grandmother's suited it and made it almost impressive. Here too she drew the curtains and went out, locking the door behind her.

Next was the sitting-room. Here she drew the curtains and looked round with momentary self-congratulation. It was a pretty and attractive room, despite its bad proportions. It was slightly too high for its size, but the height of the bookcase-bureau and of the wing-back chairs, even the size of the branches of tawny beech-leaves on a plant-stand more than averagely tall, did much to conceal this fault.

Leaving this room she did not lock the door behind her. The telephone was there. Exactly at seven-thirty

Hal would make his faithful, punctual call and if she had to fiddle about with keys he'd think she had broken a leg or something. Anyway, this room was all right. The other one, the empty one, across the hall, she hated. It had french windows, with no curtains; it was starkly empty with nothing to distract the eye, or the attention for a second. "A good place for children," she had said, eight months ago. But now there it was, empty. Harmless. She backed out of it, closed and locked the door.

At the foot of the stairs she switched on the light that illuminated the landing, and with a mixture of cringing and bravado went up to inspect that floor. Their own bedroom, and a guest-room, both pretty; bathroom, as spanking new as the kitchen; the little room where Hal had worked, when he brought work home; a table, a chair, a shelf of technical books, a cupboard where he kept clothes not much in use; and the fourth room; some suitcases and boxes; the golf clubs he had never used at Ashforth because he had been too busy reclaiming the long-neglected garden. Nothing else, except the big old looking-glass, broken when they moved, which, like the kitchen window, had once given her a fright.

She locked that door too. All was well, so far. Nobody in the house but herself. Of that she was certain; but the feeling of being watched, under a close and hostile inspection which made mock of the locked doors and the drawn curtains, went with her, down the stairs, into the kitchen. There she prepared her tray; a crust of bread, some cheese, teacup, milk. She hated filling the kettle, the sound of the running water interfered with her wary listening; but she did it, the tap turned to a dribble; then she watched the kettle, ready to catch it before it could make its glupping, boiling noise. She caught it exactly and was pouring the boiling water over the tea in the pot when something rapped at the window. She gave a great start and some of the water splashed over on to her left hand.

Yet she *knew* what had tapped on the window: a branch of the jasmine bush which, when she and Hal had come to look at the house, eight months ago, had almost occluded the kitchen window. Hal had cut it back, practically to the root, and so far from resenting this treatment, it had responded valiantly, sending out long flexible branches. In the summer the scent had come in at the open window. The bush was bare now and when a spray touched the window it sounded like a finger tapping. The wind was rising, she thought as she smeared ointment over the scald. Windy nights were always full of the most extraordinary noises: one could not listen properly.

She carried the tray into the sitting-room and sat down in the chair nearest the telephone, twisting the chair slightly so that her back was to the wall. She felt better in that position. She drank the tasteless tea, forced down the bread and cheese, indistinguishable from one another, and waited, listening.

She had always been a great reader, able to sit down with a book and lose herself, forgetting time and place, forgetting even her oven, but a book was no solace now. Her eye conveyed nothing to her mind. The television was useless, too, since with it on she could not hear. She could, however, knit, and she did so, almost frenziedly, pausing now and then to look at the door, at the window; and to listen. At the same time she

tried to force herself to be calm; she must be calm
and under control when the telephone rang. She knew
that if in any way she gave Hal the slightest inkling
of what had happened, of the secret she was keeping
from him, he'd jump straight into the car and come
home.

Although she was waiting for it when the telephone
rang, she started, dropped some stitches.

"Hullo, honey; how are you?"

"Fine, darling. And you?"

"Busy as the devil. I know everybody says poor old
Stubbs died *suddenly*, but by the state of things here
you'd think he'd been dead a year. Still, I'm pressing
on. Any news?"

"Four lots today. One couple wanted a bungalow—
so why did they come? Two bijou-residence types, I
could tell at a glance. And one rather grand. You
know. What, no downstairs cloakroom! What, only
one garage! But never mind; there is another client
tomorrow. A man with five children looking for a
family house! Even if the five should be all of one sex,
which is unlikely, the four bedrooms should appeal to
him, don't you think?"

"Let's hope so. Honey, I'll be home Friday night . . ."

"*This* Friday? The day after tomorrow? Darling, you
said a month, three weeks at least. This very Friday?"

"There are certain advantages to being boss-boy."

"Darling, how marvellous! It has seemed an age."

"To me too. Well, honey, look after yourself. Sure
you're all right?"

"Right as rain. Or a trivet. Take your pick."

They exchanged a few more irrelevant remarks.
They said goodnight, fondly. Dropping the receiver

back at his end he thought that she sounded in cracking good form. Cradling hers she felt a feeling of achievement; she had not given herself away. And she was now free to go, scuttle up the stairs, into her bedroom which though it did not offer *positive* safety did seem, after dark, the safest place of all. And once in it she had no need to go out again. The bathroom opened out of it. In the bathroom she swallowed two, and then, after a moment's thought, a third aspirin. What she needed, and she knew it, was a sound night's sleep.

That she could not keep watch, or listen while asleep, did not occur to her; all she needed at the moment was a blotting out of consciousness, an end of fear. Being in bed helped, the solid mattress under her, the blanket drawn up high gave a feeling of security; spurious, she knew that, but it served. She slept. And woke with a start. This is it! She reared up, sweating.

Nothing. Nothing but the wind. And the contraction of old floorboards as the thermostat, faithful as Hal, switched off, and the water pipes cooled. No, there was a third noise, less easily identified and explained, a furtive creaking, sporadic. Exactly the sound of someone opening a window, an inch at a time and pausing after each creak, wondering if the noise had been heard. The sound came from the bathroom where a new, metal-framed window had been fitted.

For a moment she could do nothing but cower in the bed, certain that this was the personification of all her vague fears; somebody, something, nameless and faceless, attempting to break in by the bathroom window. Her heart was behaving in such a way and breath was so difficult to draw that she thought she was dying. Then something else took over. It might be a burglar, a simple ordinary housebreaker, attracted by the *For Sale* notice. He would have brought the ladder from the potting shed, or have climbed up the drainpipe; in either case as he inched open the window his stance would be precarious and for some seconds he would be vulnerable to surprise attack, one resolute thrust. She was now in the grip of the self-preservative fear under the impact of which the victim can run faster, jump higher, perform deeds of reckless valour. She could reach out, switch on her bedside lamp, get out of bed, tear open the bathroom door, and rush to the window, fully prepared to push a man to certain injury, perhaps to death.

The window was securely latched, just as she had left it; and outside there was nothing but the night. Yet the stealthy creaking went on; it was now behind her. A trick, she thought, whirling round.

The noise came from the waste-paper-basket under the wash-bowl, into which she had thrown the crunched-up cellophane paper in which a box of soap tablets had been sealed. It was slowly but surely releasing itself from the ball shape into which she had squeezed it. As she watched, it moved a little and emitted another creak.

She began to laugh, recognised the note of hysteria, and thought—*I must not!* Then she felt, and presently was, sick. She thought—*There go the aspirins*. In the cupboard over the basin there were six or seven real sedatives, prescribed by the doctor for Hal when digging and rooting out stumps had provoked a sharp attack of sciatica. She had sent for the doctor in panic, convinced that Hal had slipped a disc and unless attended to, would be a cripple for life. Both Hal and the doctor had thought she was a fuss-pot. But there the pills were and she was tempted. But they must be saved. "To be taken only on the night before Hal comes home," the self-written invisible direction said. So that when he arrived she could face him with her ordinary, well-sleep-nourished face. So that he never guessed; never knew what an absolutely howling mistake she had made, how wrong her judgement had been; what an absolute fool she was and how she was being punished. Tomorrow she would take a proper pill and sleep. Tonight more aspirin. She went back to bed, listening, knitted a little, tried and abandoned the crossword; dozed, woke. This was now the pattern of her days and her nights.

On Thursday Hal rang, as usual, and presently asked, "What of the man with the five children?"

"Oh, they liked it. It is those stairs down to the kitchen. The wife said, very reasonably, that seven couldn't eat in our dining niche and using the dining-room she did need a place where a trolley could run between stove and table. I saw her point."

So did he; it was an awkward, inconvenient bastard of a house, and but for Meg he would never have given it a thought.

"Anyway," he said, "I'll be back tomorrow. As near eight as I can make it."

"Drive carefully," she said. She always said that. She did not drive herself. He had tried to teach her. In handling the controls she had been dexterous, but at a right-hand turn or a roundabout she'd dither. "It never seems my turn to go." Then, with a long line of angry, held-up drivers hooting behind her, she would launch out, bang in the path of an oncoming lorry. He had

had some hair-raising moments before he gave the verdict: "Honey, you're constitutionally unfit to drive a car."

He would also have said that she was constitutionally unfit to live in a house alone. Imagination was a thing he had little of, but he recognised it, in her. Once in a high wind she said, "It always sounds to me like lost souls crying." And of thunder, "You can see, can't you, why people thought of it as the voice of an angry god." And when some sap gathered on the stump of a bush he had cut down, she had put her finger to it and said, "Poor thing; its lifeblood." Her unshakable decision to stay at Ashforth, to keep the house looking pretty and occupied until it was sold, had astounded him. Worried him, too.

He was far from reckless, but he was a forceful driver, always making it his turn to go, and on Friday he was home well before eight. He ran the car into the garage and went up the path between the lilacs and laurels, guided by the rosy glow of the kitchen window. He put his key into the door, turned it, and was checked by the chain. Sensible girl! He should have thought of such a precaution; but he had left in a hurry.

"Hi! Meg! Honey! It's me."

She had been unlocking doors, making everything seem usual; given another few minutes she would have re-started the grandfather clock.

She let him in and flung herself at him. He was reminded of an exuberant puppy he had once owned. He hugged her with considerable fervour, too, and then said, "Honey, you're thinner. Have you been eating properly?"

"Oh yes. Huge meals every day." But she was thinner, every feature sharpened: she looked like some-one just recovering from an illness. He mentioned it again and she said, "It's all this exercise. Upstairs, downstairs, in my lady's chamber. This way to the garage. Any more for the potting shed? Average four a day. Guaranteed to work off the suet."

"What's wrong with your hand?"

"Oh!" She appeared to be disconcerted by this natural question. "J . . . just a drop of hot water."

What he thought of as a "funny" look was in evidence again later; once in the hall when he said, "Hullo! Grandfather stopped?"

She was guiltily aware of the weights she had re-moved and which now lay inside at the bottom of the clock. For such deliberate sabotage there was no ex-planation. She coloured.

"Don't bother with that now," she said and almost pulled him into the sitting-room. And there he picked up her book. He very seldom read novels but he liked to make a show of sharing her interests and he had a memory like a computer.

"Still on this?" he said in a surprised way.

She almost snatched it.

"It isn't a b . . . book to read quickly."

Then the sight of the television set reminded him of the serial they had been watching.

"I've had no time to watch," he said. "Who did murder that girl?"

"I don't know. It was all such a m . . . muddle. I couldn't be b . . . bothered."

As she spoke she remembered that it was the ex-ceptional clarity of that thriller that had endeared it to them. She wondered how people managed with a really *guilty* secret to hide.

After that they spent their usual happy evening.

When they went up to bed Hal took his case, and intending not to clutter up the pretty bedroom, turned to the little room. The door was locked. If she'd had half a dozen lovers hidden away there she couldn't have looked more confused, more caught out. The explanation came out, too promptly, too glibly.

"I locked it. M . . . Monday night. It was very windy. That door j . . . j . . . juddered. So I locked it and it stopped. And I didn't need to g . . . go in. So . . ."

In the morning, after an excellent night's sleep, the first for almost a fortnight, she slipped down, replaced the weights on the clock, and re-started it. Lucky for once, she thought. She had stopped it in the evening, just before seven, and now it was morning, just before seven, so there were no irrelevant chimes to attract attention. It was not even mentioned.

Saturday was a splendid day; and so was Sunday, until lunch time. Roast beef at one o'clock and Hal had said he need not leave until nine. That left eight hours before the torment began again.

As though he sensed it—and she gave him his due, where she was concerned he was surprisingly sensitive —Hal said, "Meg, how about coming back with me? It's only a pub, but it's comfortable. We could shove the keys and a note into old Treadman's office on our way out and *he* could show people round."

She wanted to do it so much, so violently, so madly,

that the effort to resist the almost irresistible temptation brought an ugly rasping note into her voice.

"Let's not go through all that again. I may not be clever, but I do know about houses. And I know that a house, with somebody in it, and flowers about, and a fire is far more saleable . . . I said, didn't I, that I should stay here until . . . and just because it's been a fortnight . . . It's a hopeless house. I took to it, though, and somebody else will. You'll see. After all, what's a fortnight?"

"Well," he said, "let's hope you're right.

She said, in a voice more like her own, "And the minute it is sold, I shall catch the first train."

She saw that moment, a light at the end of a long tunnel. But there was another moment, coming up on panther feet.

He had his coat, two books, the business section of the Sunday paper, and his case. Any normal loving wife would carry something and go with him to the garage door; but if she locked the back door behind her he would guess: if she did not lock it she would be obliged to return to a house that had been left unguarded. She eyed the bushes with suspicion.

"I won't come out," she said with a simulated shudder. "It's turned a bit c . . . cold."

He put down everything and embraced her. Her greeting had been puppyish; now her clutch reminded him of that of a boy he'd once saved from drowning.

"Take care of yourself," he said. "I'll ring tomorrow; usual time." He wasn't three paces from the door before he heard the lock snap down and the chain rattle into place.

Seventy miles solitary driving gave a man time to think.

There were no flowers left in the garden; but her dried hydrangea heads and some red berries looked well on the hall chest. Instead of the posy, some wax fruit, under a glass dome, graced the dining table—a real period piece. Nobody came.

"Any news?" Hal asked as usual.

"A couple came—at least I think they did. Mr. Treadman said . . . And I saw a c . . . c . . . car outside, quite a long t . . . time. Two people. They stared and then drove off."

"Well, I have news for you! I heard of a house this morning and went to look at it at lunch time. *Rather* nice, I think, and sure to sell at once. But I can't decide without you, can I? Could you come tomorrow and give it the once over?"

Desperation, envy of people with a house so easily saleable, angry with Hal for being so silly, made her almost incoherent. Stammering badly she demanded to know how he could think of looking at a house with this one still unsold. What would they use for money?

He said, "Hold on! We have a house that will sell, eventually. And with my present job . . . We could get a mortgage." She saw this house abandoned, growing more unsaleable with every passing day and the mortgage a great black burden for years. Almost ferociously, the stammer growing wilder, she told him that that was not the way to do things. Aware of the space that ached emptily away behind the locked doors, trying to listen as she talked, shooting wary little glances

about, she told Hal that she would not b . . . b . . .
budge until this house was sold.

That was Monday. On Tuesday Mr. Treadman
telephoned to say that he was sending a *likely* couple;
they were not interested in new properties. They looked
likely; but when she opened the door to them she
was stammering so badly that she could hardly point
out the good features—the staggeringly efficient and
economical boiler; the joy of being able to look into
the garden as you worked at the sink; the plentitude of
cupboard space.

("I did like it," the woman in the mink hat and coat
said, "until I stepped inside. The moment I did I knew
it had the wrong atmosphere. There's something badly
wrong in that house. She knows it, too." The husband
said, "For its size and condition it seemed cheap. You
could be right." They agreed that it was a pity.)

She had now remembered the old trick of dealing
with a stammer. The elusive word must be abandoned,
another one hastily substituted and caught before it
could escape. She had learned the trick in a sweetshop.
Butterscotch a hurdle not to be taken; fruit drops
presenting no difficulty at all. She had outgrown the
stammer when she was eleven, but she remembered
the trick.

In answer that evening to Hal's routine inquiry, she
employed it.

' "Only one c . . . c . . . a man and a woman.
N . . . n . . . pleasant. She was all m . . . m . . .
ermine. R . . . r . . . wealthy, but no g . . . g . . .
useless. I c . . . c . . . Knew . . ."

On Wednesday, just before midday, Mr. Treadman telephoned.

"Mrs. Beverly?"

"Y . . . y . . . Speaking."

"I hope you will be happy to know that I have had an offer for your house. A firm, definite offer."

She made a noise which, in the circumstances, he took to indicate delight.

"H . . . h . . . Which ones?" Despite all, she was fond of the house and wanted to know into whose hands it had fallen.

"Nobody I sent. In fact my client is not in this area at all. But we send out particulars, you know. This gentleman is known to me—slightly. I can assure you that he will not back out, or change his mind."

"Th . . . th . . . I'm very gr . . . gr . . . thank-ful, Mr. Treadman."

Disregarding her own strict rule about not disturbing Hal at the office, she dialled the number and gasped out the good news. "So I can c . . . c . . . get on the t . . . t . . . next train."

"The two-thirty. Splendid I'll meet you. And Meg," he had visions of her falling downstairs with a suitcase, running to catch a bus, and getting knocked down, "just be calm. Pack an overnight bag. Ring for a taxi."

She said, hardly stammering at all, "Darling, the irony! Here I've been, going through h . . . h . . . hell to keep it looking lived in, and now somebody has b . . . b . . . taken it, sight unseen." She began to laugh: but even in the quality of the laughter there was a disquieting note that convinced him that he had done the right thing; the only possible thing. Ahead lay the subterfuges and the financial juggling required of a man who had just "bought" his own house in Ashford and intended to buy another in Wisborough: but he had a calm and equable nature and could face such trivialities without dismay.

The Big Bed of Bad Pyrmont

Everything about this affair is touched with absurdity; even the way in which I discovered the fact that Mark, whom I trusted absolutely, had been unfaithful to me for four years.

He tries to be independent about money and, to help to pay his share of the holiday we planned later on, had taken a job lecturing at a summer school, and I snatched the opportunity of having his study redecorated. This meant moving the heavy, handsome, eighteenth-century writing table which I'd given him, years ago, as a birthday present. I stood by while the two men wrestled with it, admonishing one another,

"Up your end!" "Now, heave!" "Steady there!" One of them must have touched a spring, for a flap in the panelling at the side sprang open and some letters fell out, face downwards, at my feet.

I thought they were mine, the ones I had sent him in that terrible year when the whole of my family were doing their damnedest to make me change my mind about marrying him. How sweet, how like him to have kept them, remindful as they must be of a time of uncertainty for him. Then, as I stooped, I saw the poor quality of the paper. Cheap stuff.

Even in a crisis, what you have been brought up to do or not to do counts. Before I'd read a word I felt soiled; reading other people's letters, unthinkable! But I read them, every word, and learned that for the last four years I had been sharing my husband with a girl named Emma who taught in a small place about ten miles on the other side of town. Then I felt sick. I was sick. I was sick on and off all day. One of the painters said it must be the smell of paint; it took some people like that, he said.

Yet the letters in themselves were delightful, full of humour and kindness, never a whine or a demand; there were quotations, references to books that she had enjoyed, or found a bit beyond her. The general tone was humble and grateful and any mention of their love-making made in euphemistic, almost poetical, terms. A thoroughly nice girl, this Emma. But when you are stabbed to the heart the character of the one who holds the knife is not important. You are stabbed.

The worst thing, at first, was the feeling of utter humiliation, the knowledge that one had been so thoroughly fooled. I'd never known Mark to look at another woman in that way in the fifteen and a half years we'd been married. I'd have sworn that his ideas on marital fidelity were strict, partly the result of his blood, which is German-Jewish in origin, of his class, most respectably bourgeois; and partly the result of his nature, which is so honest that he would never indulge in that mild sycophancy which is sometimes necessary for success. Twice, to my knowledge, his honesty had resulted in his being passed over by men of far less merit; and it is typical of him that he spent ten years writing quite a small book because every fact must be checked, re-examined, and re-assessed and before he could write ten words he must read ten thousand. Painfully honest, utterly frank, I would have said. Yet he'd deceived me for four years.

And there was nothing wrong, so far as I could see, with our marriage, or with me. Admittedly I'm not intellectual, but I know when to be quiet and I am a good hostess, because that was a thing I was schooled to be. Even Mark's most egg-headed friends, the ones who talk about the incomprehensible originality of Kafka, have always seemed to enjoy my hospitality, the good food and wine, the comfort which money alone can provide. At thirty-five I still had looks—there again money helps. Why? Why had this happened to me?

I've always been scrupulous about disturbing Mark either at the university or when he was working at home, and even on this terrible day I waited until five o'clock before getting in touch with him. He was surprised to hear my voice. "Helen! Is anything wrong?"

"Yes," I said. "You must come home." My voice sounded thin. "I want you to come home."

"Your mother?" he asked. Mother has a heart condition.

"No. It's nothing like that."

"Then what? Darling, you sound very upset."

"I am. I have to talk to you." *Why? Why? Why?*

There was a little pause, perhaps half a minute, and I could imagine his face as his mind went into action, weighing up the situation, making the decision. Then he said, "Helen, whatever it is, it is all right. I'm on my way."

That set me crying; it was said so comfortingly, in his deep reliable voice; and it made me remember the times when he had comforted me, often over silly little things. In families like mine a great value is put on courage and self-control; it was a new and pleasant thing for me to find that Mark didn't find my dread of spiders and mice a matter for fun. And now he was rushing home through the summer evening, intent upon putting right whatever was wrong. Something that could never be put right.

I cried myself silly. Then I had to pull myself together, because by half-past ten, the earliest he could arrive, he'd be starving; he's a man who attaches great value to food. I started preparations for a meal, setting the table and so on. The very sight of food made me sicken again and my hands shook so much they were almost useless; I kept dropping things; I broke a glass. I thought of brandy being good for shock and drank some. After a time it steadied me a little and it changed my mood; the awful feeling of humiliation lifted a bit and gave way to anger. Also the question "Why" yielded to the question "When?" How had he found time to lead this double life?

I forced myself to go through the letters again. Actually the bed-thing was not mentioned more than about half a dozen times: "the memory of last night will stay with me for ever"; "your being able to stay on Thursday was the most lovely birthday present any-one could have." Things like that. I looked at post-marks and routed out my old diaries. True enough. "Mark at X or Y or Z," meaning evening lectures at places far enough away to justify his not getting home. "Mark at dinner for Dr. A, Professor B, Mr. C." Mark in bed with Emma! These were occasions I could trace directly; but three times when Mother was at the point of death, by her own reckoning, I'd gone home and he'd come down for week-ends. And Emma might not always have mentioned . . . No matter, half a dozen or a hundred; once was enough!

Anger is more bearable than shame or bereavement. I gulped down another brandy and became very angry indeed, and quite steady. I'll show him, I thought, what he's traded in for this country schoolteacher! I went into the garden and got great sheaves of flowers, not cutting them carefully as I usually do, but hacking and slashing. I'm good with flowers and I set huge, glowing arrangements everywhere, as though for a party. I put out a bottle of his favourite claret; how much Mouton Rothschild will you be able to afford on your wretched little salary? How well can Emma cook? And what will she look like when she's thirty-five? There's no substitute for youth—and the letters sounded young—but she would not be young for ever.

Mark is forty-one; before my family knew that I was serious, he was known as "your fat friend." He wasn't fat then, except by comparison with all the lean, stringy men we knew, but it has crept upon him lately. And he's one of those men who, to be presentable in the evening, must shave again. By half-past ten, when he arrived, his chin and the lower part of his cheeks looked very dark, especially as the upper part of his face and his forehead, from which the hair is receding, looked pale from the strain of a headlong drive. And being away from me for four days and treating his clothes as he does, he looked . . . scruffy. Ageing, fattening, balding, scruffy. It should have been easy. It wasn't. At the sight of him, hurrying in with that somehow buoyant tread some heavy men have, my real impulse was to throw myself at him, to say, "Oh Mark, something dreadful has happened!" to lean against him and be comforted.

His expression, anxious to start with—usually I met him at the door and heaven knows what he had been thinking—brightened with relief when he saw me there, standing strong on my feet, not in any obvious distress. Would you think that a man with such a candid face could be such an expert deceiver? Never a whisper, never a misplaced word. He's cleverer than I am. After the relief of seeing me all right he sensed the tension and said, coming towards me, "Whatever it is, darling, it's all right now. I'm here."

He came to give me the usual hug and kiss. What with one thing and another, I hadn't thought of that. In my anger I'd planned that he should eat and drink and then be told. I wasn't thinking straight at all. Completely muddled. But as he came towards me I said, "Don't touch me. I know about Emma!"

Well, it was stab for stab. There are degrees of pallor. For a second I thought he was going to die. He said, "Oh dear." There was a chair handy; he dropped into it as though somebody had hit him at the back of the knees. And there he sat, looking at me exactly like a beagle puppy I once had who never could cotton on to the idea of house training, but knew when he'd offended. "Who told you?"

"These," I said, and slapped the letters down on the table.

He looked relieved. No gossip; just a dirty little secret between him and me. "There's nothing I can say. Except that I'd have given an arm rather than have you know."

"I'd have given two rather than have it happen!"

"You'd better know the end of it," he said, and fumbled inside his jacket and took out another, similar letter and held it towards me. I took it and read it, all in one gulp as though I'd taken one of those rapid reading courses. She'd known in her heart it was all wrong . . . blamed herself . . . the only thing to do was to get away so when you read this . . . some really worthwhile work in one of those underprivileged places half a world away.

"Splendid! That makes two lives you've ruined."

"God, I hope not!" He put his hand over his eyes for a second. "The thing is," he said, "and a thing you must try to understand, Helen, that never once, not for a minute did I stop loving . . ."

"Don't give me that old rot! I can just see you hopping into bed with Emma with a placard round your neck—I love Helen."

"You have every right to be angry. But in a way

that is true. If you look back"—he spoke almost pains-takingly, as though explaining a difficult theory to a stupid student—"on no single occasion did I put her first; the nights I . . . spent there were ones I should have spent away in any case."

"You think that helps?" I said furiously. "You make me sick! When I think of the times when you must have come straight from her to me . . ."

"That I never did," he said, quickly. "Helen, please, please, credit me at least with a little . . . taste."

"Oh, with more than that. I credit you with being the best double dealer of the century. What I want to know, why I asked you to come, is *why?* Everything's always been all right between us, so far as I know. I'm not academic, but you knew that when you married me. I can see that your Emma is a nice girl, a kindred spirit, all those quotations. . . . *But why did you have to go to bed with her?*"

I could see the computer set to work. "I suppose," he said, "because man is not a monogamous animal. And she bolstered my self-esteem."

Something exploded in my head. I began to shake again and heard my voice—not mine, the voice of a hysterical virago—using words we all know but properly-brought-up people do not use. Then his hands were on my shoulders.

"Darling, don't. You don't know what you're say-ing." He smelt the brandy, I suppose. "You've been drinking on an empty stomach. Let me get you some-thing to eat."

That infuriated me still more. "Your cure for every-thing; a good guzzle! All this bloody highmindedness and the mysticism of Blake. Phony as hell! It all boils down to getting a bellyful and then a roll in the hay with the first little tart that is ready and willing. Take your hands off me."

He stood back and looked at me solemnly.

He said, "I don't think you're in a condition to make a major decision, but of course, if you want to divorce me . . ."

I'd never thought as far as that; I hadn't had time. And although I had drunk more than I usually do, I wasn't as intoxicated as he chose to believe. Divorce; and the whole of my family down to the last second cousin saying, "But, of course, I always said it could never work."

I said, "I haven't yet decided what to do. I need time to think things over. I think I shall go to Germany." I said the last word viciously. We'd spent vacations in various countries in Europe, but never Germany. Some of his family had gone to the gaschambers there in the thirties.

Except for the misery that I carried about with me like a cancer and the nagging need to make up my mind, I should have enjoyed the trip. As it was, I missed Mark at every turn. I could hardly eat anything, but I never sat down to table without thinking: *How Mark would have revelled in this*. And whenever I joined a tour to some ancient place I was haunted by the thought of how, in other countries, he had always had some story or piece of information that made the dead stones live.

The curious thing was that the more I missed Mark, the angrier I became, and the more I hated Emma. The person who robs you of a diamond offends you

more than one who makes away with a bit of a costume
jewellery. I knew where Mark was; we'd had a couple
of painfully stilted talks over the telephone before I
left, and he was holding to his schedule. I was lost,
wandering hither and thither following whims or sug-
gestions.

It was at the suggestion of another similar wanderer
that I took a day trip to a place called Bad Pyrmont.
It is very old, it is very pretty, but really there is
nothing to hold one there even for a day. There's a
picturesque street, lined with old houses and pollarded
chestnut trees, a medieval *Schloss*, a well-laid-out
public garden, and that is all. But for me it had something, an appeal there was no accounting for. I ra-
tionalised; it would be a good place in which to do
some serious thinking; as I must.

I decided to stay for a day or two.

There was nothing very much to do. I walked about,
tried to think; thoughts of reconciliation brought up
short by disgust, thoughts of divorce by dismay. Weren't
you warned? Didn't we try to dissuade you? Once my
father said to me, "What I fail to see is what on
earth you'll find to *talk* about. Now your mother and I
don't see alike on any subject, but we can always talk
about dogs and horses. What'll you have?" They'd
gloat. On the other hand . . .

I ended up towards the end of the afternoon in the
little local museum, a few well-kept, well-arranged
rooms in a tall, ancient house. Agricultural tools, old
weapons, pottery, a few pictures of no great value or
interest. A party of people, all German, were being
led round by the curator. I tried to keep apart from

them but, since he was explaining as he went and I was just idly looking, I caught up with them in an upstairs room in which the main exhibit was a great bed, rather ugly, roughly but solidly made, about eight feet square. There was obviously some tale about it, which the curator enjoyed telling. When you don't understand a word, you take notice of facial expressions. His, when he ended his tale, said, "There! What do you think of that?" Most people laughed; a young woman with a baby on her arm smiled, but looked astonished and a bit dubious; a man gave the footboard of the bed an approving pat.

They trooped out and I stood aside. The curator said to me—in English—how *do* they know?—"Madam is interested in the big bed of Pyrmont?"

"Well," I said, "it certainly is big."

"Made so," he said, "with purpose. I will tell you."

So he told me. The gist was this. Some time in the Middle Ages a knight from the *Schloss*—"Madam has seen the *Schloss* by the river?"—went on a Crusade, leaving his wife behind in charge of everything. A bad neighbour tried to take advantage of the knight's absence to take his castle and his land. The wife fought him off. Six years passed and the knight was reckoned dead. He'd never reached the Holy Land, having been taken prisoner by the Turks and thrown into a dungeon. But his captor had a daughter who fell in love with the prisoner and presently organised his escape. He couldn't leave her behind to be thrown into the Bosporus, so he brought her home with him. "And here, one sees, is the problem. To one side the good wife who is saving his castle and bringing up his children for six years, to the other side the good girl who is risking her life to save him. Which to choose? So he has made this big bed and together in it they sleep for many years."

I suppose that all through the summer he told that tale twice a day at least, but he looked at me, asking that I should laugh. I managed a perfunctory smile and said, "It is a charming story."

"Is also a true story," he said with some reproach.

Outside it was hot. I went and sat at a café table under the shade of one of the chestnut trees, and ordered tea with lemon. I thought about the silly little story, probably legendary; or, if true, so old as to have nothing to do with life as we know it; set in a barbarous time. But, of course, there were the obvious similarities, the triangular situation, the fact that one man had kept two women happy—as Mark had done for four years. There was also the obvious difference: the knight's wife had sound good reason to be grateful to the Turkish girl. Whereas I . . .

Then it hit me. Thinking that I had no reason to be grateful to Emma, I remembered something that Mark had said which I had passed over at the time. "And she bolstered my self-esteem." I thought of the knocks his self-esteem had taken, seeing them clearly for the first time. That terrible year, enough to undermine any man, then the patronising acceptance; all the provision made for me so poor Helen didn't suffer materially from her mis-mating. Even the house wasn't his choice, he hadn't wanted to live so far out, but my father was paying for it, what did Mark's wish matter? Professionally he wasn't successful, passed over twice, but thinking everything would change once his book was finished, he'd had such hopes for it. And it was a flop, almost unnoticed and the sales microscopic. I, God forgive me, had once said, meaning to comfort him, "Never mind, darling; it isn't as though we needed the money!" That was just four years ago. That was when he began taking extra-mural engagements. That was when he met Emma. And if she hadn't rescued him from a dungeon, she'd rescued him from feeling a failure, helped him over the hump. She'd saved him for me, kept him sweet and cheerful, loving and kind, lovable and sane. I had a good deal to thank Emma for. I still couldn't go so far as to feel that I'd share him with her in the present or the future but, once I understood, I could forget the past.

Later on, of course, I realised that I was so lonely and miserable and undecided that almost anything would have triggered me off, one way or the other. It was my good luck that there happened to be, in Pyrmont, this absurd big bed.

Man in a Dilemma

Now and again you see a play, or read a book in which some utterly trivial incident precipitates a scene during which the characters suddenly reveal thoughts, feelings, and grievances that they have concealed for years. Whenever this happens I always think—*Well, thank God, nothing like that could go on between Nancy and me.* She wouldn't wait ten minutes, leave alone ten years, to tell me that the popping noise I made when lighting my pipe exasperated her past bearing. She is forthright to the point of bluntness. This can be uncomfortable, even embarrassing at times, but at least you know where you are.

In June of this year I was offered a post which meant an increase of salary and brighter prospects; it also meant leaving the little house in which we had lived since we were married, and all our friends. I'm rather inclined to look at both sides of any proposition, and I might have turned down the offer, but Nancy was firm. Hadn't she always said that with my abilities I should be more ambitious? She had, repeatedly. Hadn't she always said that my chance must come? As for the house, it was now worth more than we had given for it; and surely to goodness we could find a house in Charrington. As for friends, were we so old that we couldn't make new ones?

So letters flew to and fro, and one fine Friday afternoon, having arranged for the boys to spend a night with their school-friend, we set off for Charrington, and in the morning placed ourselves in the hands of a house agent, from whose long list of desirable properties we had already crossed off those palpably unsuited to us. We discarded without a second thought a fourteenth-century manor house with eight bedrooms, likewise a bungalow with a thirty-acre small-holding attached. Those we intended to inspect sounded feasible on paper. In fact that house agent would make a fortune if he ever turned to writing fiction.

I was unable to decide which I liked least, inspecting a house that was empty, damp, cold even on such a day, a sad house, obviously wanted by nobody; or one still in occupation, with the hopeful owners hanging about, within earshot, pathetically eager to explain that some vast Moloch of a boiler was actually very economical, and that you soon learned to duck your head under that beam. Long before midday I could see that all saleable houses in or near Charrington had been sold—probably without benefit of agents—and that those we saw empty would stay so until the process of disintegration was complete, those we saw occupied would stay inhabited by their present owners until merciful death intervened.

The agent, having failed to sell the unsaleable—and Nancy's comments anyway had been very frank—said, "Well . . ." and drove us to a house not on the list. It was fairly new, well painted, neat as a pin; the garden was small, bright with flowers; it stood in a quiet suburban road.

"Ah," I said, "this looks more like it."

"Bijou residence!" Nancy said.

I detected the scorn, but the agent said, "Exactly, madam. And the interior is even better."

I suffered, during that inspection, more than on all the others put together. The couple who lived there so obviously loved the place, had spent time and money on it, and were reluctant to leave; but he, like me, was the victim of a system that seldom brings promotion without a move. I liked the house, too, but I could see that Nancy did not. Everybody else could see it as well.

The agent, after assuring us that he had nothing else to suggest, and that he was the only one of his kind in Charrington, went jauntily on his way. We went to our hotel for lunch. Nancy spent the mealtime decrying the little house; it was even smaller than the one we now lived in, the same number of rooms but each room tinier. The boys would soon need a room apiece; and where would my books go?

"We have to have a roof over our heads by September," I said.

"Don't worry. We shall. We made a mistake saying in or near Charrington. I don't mind being in the very depth of the country. Anything rather than that super doll's house."

"Even the one with the ferns in the floorboards?"

"Of course not. That was definitely unsafe. I tell you what we'll do. We'll drive out ourselves, this afternoon. We'll ask in village post-offices. Where's the map?"

I said, "We can't do that. We promised to collect the boys by seven at latest."

"I'll give Felicity a ring. She won't mind. I had Benjy for a fortnight, don't forget."

"It was an unforgettable experience," I said.

A resolute optimist in defeat is really a piteous sight and when the resolute optimist is the woman you love, to watch her being battered, gathering herself together, and going on being resolute and optimistic, simply inviting another blow, cuts you to the heart. There were villages and in them were post-offices, manned by would-be-helpful people, almost all of whom knew of a house for sale. A lot of people knew about the manor house, though they seemed to believe that it had twelve bedrooms, not eight; the agent had conveniently ignored the attics. The name of the house with the flourishing fernery cropped up now and again, with the added comment, "Want a bit of money spent on it." But new clues were offered here and there, and Nancy, combination of bulldog and bloodhound, followed each to the bitter end. Dirty and discouraged we returned to the hotel, late for dinner, and still homeless in prospect—except of course for the bijou residence, which in all likelihood had been sold privately while we had been investigating a farmhouse, divorced from its land, but not from its piggeries or its two batteries of hens and the attendant flies.

A glass of sherry and some lukewarm food revived Nancy.

"We'll try again tomorrow," she said. "I'm sure this is the only way. After all, what could we expect? One afternoon . . ."

From far away in the past I heard an echo; a master who had tried and failed to teach me carpentry, saying, "Shelton, you give up too easily . . ." It was true. I gave up easily, I resigned myself, I settled for what was available; left to myself I should probably not have taken the job in Charrington; having taken it, left to myself, I'd now be in negotiation for the bijou residence. I lacked, to put it plainly, guts. *And perhaps,* I thought, in the clarity of complete physical and emotional exhaustion, *in Heaven, where marriages are said to be made, this fact had been recognised, and I'd been given a wife with guts enough for two.* Not a very pleasant thought, but interesting.

"We take the Penstanton road," Nancy said, "and that brings us through on to the main road home. And I've asked the hotel to give us what they call a tourist lunch. So we shan't really be wasting any time."

Penstanton St. Mary; Penstanton St. Lawrence; Penstanton St. Martin; Penstanton plain and unsanctified. Nancy simply would not give in. Village post-offices are closed on Sunday mornings, but she knocked on doors, she exerted charm, she was given direction and advice, in accordance with which I drove down rutted lanes, even across meadows and ploughed fields. She offered to take over the driving, but I, feeling some compulsion to contribute to this exercise, kept to the driver's seat and drove and drove through a whole Sunday morning which was merely the Saturday afternoon all over again. Hopeless places, either abandoned and rotting, some of them even in decay, very beautiful, places I longed to rescue—if only I had been rich! Or places so horrible, one had a corrugated iron roof, that the idea of living in them was absurd.

Every time I thought of saying, with just the right light touch, "Well, there's always the bijou residence." But I couldn't do it; it'd be too cruel. Yet, more and more, as time went on, I anchored myself to that little suburban house. I could get rid of some books; and if giving the boys a bedroom each meant that we had no spare room, what did that matter?

We ate the tourist lunch with a complete lack of the jolly vagabond spirit which alone would have made it palatable. The last leg of our futile journey had taken us directly away from the main road for which we were making and my time neurosis was beginning to work. However, it was Nancy who said, pointing on the map, "We needn't go back to Penstanton; there's a by-road. It'll be the next left-hand turn."

That was an admission of defeat and my heart bled for her. I know exactly when silence is best, however, so I said nothing; I drove, meditating in my mind how the bijou residence could be adopted on our needs; an extension to the sitting-room, an extra bedroom over the garage. I'd ring up as soon as we were home; the owner's name was Prichett and his wife had called him

Tom. I'd lose no time in making sure of the one habitable place we had seen.

Nancy said, "Stop! Bill! Stop!"

I braked, asking, "What is it?"

"That house. The one we just passed. Bill, it's empty."

"Is there a board?"

"No. But there're no curtains."

"That doesn't necessarily mean . . ." But she was gone, running back along the road in the ungainly, oddly touching manner in which women do run in high-heeled shoes. By the time I joined her she had opened the gate and was halfway along the path, studying the house with approval.

"Isn't it just what we're looking for?"

To all appearances it was; a good solid house, roomy but not rambling; plastered and painted cream, with a dark red rose climbing up one side of the front door, a yellow one on the other. The windows were without curtains, but something—the state of the garden perhaps—made me feel that this house was not unoccupied, or at least if it was it was temporarily, just the space between X moving out and Y moving in.

"It's nice enough," I said. "But we can't just march in."

"We can ring the bell," Nancy said, advancing upon the door. "If anyone answers we can explain." She gave the bell a hearty pull. The sound it made confirmed my opinion; empty houses sound empty. This one didn't.

Nobody came. Nancy began to move around to the side of the house.

"I'm going in," she said. "There never was a house

that couldn't be entered by a sufficiently determined person."

Just around the corner was a french window. She tried it; it resisted her. She cupped her hands and looked in.

"Look at that. Lined with shelves. Absolutely the room for you."

I looked. I saw the shelves. I also saw that the floor was carpeted, and that against a wall without shelves there stood a tall glass-fronted bookcase. The bell's sound had informed me rightly. This was not an empty house.

"Darling . . ." I began; but Nancy had rounded another corner, where there was a back door and beside it a kitchen window. She tried the door, looked in at the window, and said,

"What I've always wanted; a kitchen big enough to eat in."

"Darling," I said. "It is *not* an empty house. I can see a kitchen table, and a dresser. And in that other room . . . Somebody's just moving in or out. We're only tantalising . . . Oh Lord, what are you doing?" What she was doing was all too obvious; applying a nail file to the window. Very successfully, too. One half— it was a casement—opened with a sharp little crack; she reached in and opened the other half.

"Nancy, you simply can't. It's somebody's property. This is housebreaking. It's burglary!"

A flash of sleek slim legs and she was inside. Then she had the door open.

"Come in. Honestly, Bill, you look as though you have St. Vitus' Dance."

"And well I may. This is awful. How would you feel if somebody did this to our house?"

This, to me logical, question she ignored.

"For your information," she said, "burglary can only be committed by night. Does that comfort your law-abiding little soul?"

It was like a douche of icy water. Law-abiding little soul. Little. And not only the words; the voice, the look of contempt. Nancy, whom I loved, with whom I had lived happily for eleven years, had just revealed that she thought me a poor-spirited fellow. I thought of all the times, during those years, when she had said that I let myself be put upon, that I didn't make enough of myself, didn't stand up for myself. I'd always thought she spoke from affection, from a not-quite-justified esteem. Well, we live and learn.

I was now in a quandary. I wanted to say that if it pleased her to go stamping about in somebody else's house, she could do so, but I'd have no part in it. But if I did that, and went and sat in the car, she'd think I was frightened. And she would be right; damn her. I was socially, not physically frightened. We couldn't even be sure that whoever owned the house wasn't in the garden at the back, out of sound of the bell. We'd look such *fools*. However, if there should be an unpleasant situation to be faced, I must be there. I went in.

Nancy was already opening doors.

"Splendid larder." I was relieved to see that the shelves were bare. "Lovely cupboard for brooms and the Hoover. Oh, and look! Back stairs. What a blessing when the boys come in muddy." She proceeded to climb them.

As usual, I compromised. I was there, if anything

should happen, but I was not sharing this pipe-dream.
The kitchen faced north and even on this summer day
was chilly; but through an inner door I could see a
square hall, with a window and a window-seat, full in
the sun. I moved into position there and lighted a
cigarette. Overhead I could hear Nancy galloping
about like a pony. When she came clattering downstairs she gave me a breathless report, as though I had
asked her for it. My detachment she completely ignored.

"Four bedrooms, one with a four-poster. And the
bathroom is quite modern. Now I'm going into the
garden. I think there are fruit trees." She unbolted the
half-glazed door just to the left of where I sat and
went out. She wasn't interested in whether I went with
her or not; she hadn't noticed that since entering the
house I hadn't said a word; she was blissfully oblivious
to the significance of the four-poster bed. She was like
a bird trying to build a nest in some impossible place.
Bird-brain, I said to myself, *nit-wit, daft!*

She'd been gone less than half a minute when the
thing I'd dreaded all along happened. Somewhere
above my head a voice asked, "Is anybody there?"
It was a female voice, very assured and haughty, the
voice of precisely the kind of person by whom one
would wish not to be caught in any dubious or un-
conventional act. My face went hot, my hands and
feet cold. I looked up and saw the owner of the
voice emerge from one of the bedroom doors, cross
the landing, and begin to descend the stairs. Old, short,
stout, but upright and light on her feet. Queen Victoria
to the life, even to the jowls that sagged under the pale,
squarish face. Her expression was far from friendly.

I stood up, and with the old army skill slipped my cigarette into my pocket and squeezed it out.

"And what, may I ask, are you doing in my house?"

I have been told that I possess, when I care to exert it, a certain charm. Exerting it to cracking point, I explained, apologised, making very free with the "ma'am's." A bit of my mind slid off and thought—This'll teach Nancy! Prove I was right for once.

The old woman relented at last.

"Well, it sounds rather an *odd* thing to do. When I found the back door open and the door to the back stairs, I was afraid it might be *boys*. They've been a great nuisance. I'm obliged to come in almost every day, and it's quite a long walk."

She sat down in the place where I had been.

"Well, Mr. . . . ?"

"Shelton. Bill Shelton."

"I'm Mrs. Bulmer." There was that inexplicable, uneasy silence that follows any introduction. "So youre interested in my house?"

"Is it for sale?"

"That depends entirely upon who wishes to buy it. I did place it in an agent's hands, but of course he was concerned only with his commission; and my nephew, who is supposed to *help* me with my affairs, entirely lacks discrimination. You may think me unduly sentimental, but this was my home; for forty years. One becomes attached."

"I can understand that. I should feel the same." Indeed I did feel the same about leaving the place where I'd lived for eleven years.

"It isn't as though I'd moved away and couldn't see

what was going on. I'm just in the village and should know if it fell into the hands of awful people."

She looked me up and down with that calculating stare that makes you wonder about your buttons. Exactly how awful did I seem to her?

"There's another thing, too. Such pieces of furniture as are too large for my present limited accommodation. They're old-fashioned, but sound and good, and I'm asking very little for them; but they must remain. Would that be agreeable to you?"

I said, "You mean . . . you're willing to sell the house to us? Oh, Mrs. Bulmer, how wonderful! It's exactly what we were looking for. I must tell Nancy!" My fit of spleen forgotten, I took a step towards the door.

Mrs. Bulmer said, "Wait. I'm a little short of time at the moment." She stood up and looked at her watch, a large gold one, meant to be worn on a chain, converted to wear on the wrist by being inserted into a clumsy leather case. "I can see her from here, one can always judge."

Nancy was at the very end of the back garden, amongst some fruit trees. She appeared to be in a trance; and she looked as neat and trim and as far from awful as any woman could. Mrs. Bulmer's verdict was, however, on the grudging side.

"She looks very capable," she said.

"She is," I said. "Most capable. She's probably planning apple jelly. . . ." Too eager; it sounded as though I were giving Nancy a reference. "Now, with whom do I get in touch, to discuss price and such details?"

Had she been a little less formidable I'd have asked

her outright what she was asking; for already this seemed too good to be true. The snag might well lie in the price.

"I suppose it's still on Mr. Kenyon's books," she said, naming the agent with whom we had spent Saturday morning. "I really must go now." She stretched out a plump white hand, and I took it. At close range she gave off a sweet, desiccated scent, like old potpourri. "This has been a most fortunate encounter. I hope you'll be happy here. You'll lock up? Leave by the front door; it has a Yale lock."

She moved towards the door of the kitchen, halted there, and half-turned.

"Oh, by the way, Mr. . . . er . . . Shelton. You need have no fear that I shall always be on your doorstep. Once I'm assured that the place is in suitable hands, I shall be glad to be spared the walk."

With another kind of woman one could have said that of course she'd be welcome, that we'd want her to see what we made of it, that I'd fetch her in the car. But there was something inhibiting about her manner; even Nancy would recognise that when they met. So I said nothing but went racing into the garden to tell Nancy my wonderful news.

It wasn't taken in the right spirit. For a full ten minutes, the time it took to look over the garden and the whole house again, Nancy was pointing out how right she had been, how wrong I was. But for her we should never have seen the house, never have entered it, never made contact with Mrs. Bulmer. This was strictly true, but I felt that I deserved a crumb of credit for the way I had handled an awkward situation. It was, after all, my behaviour that had convinced the old dame that we were suitable people. Nancy spoke as though she had breasted a stormy sea, heavily handicapped by my inert weight, and managed—just—to pull us both safe ashore. There was nothing new in this attitude, but being called a little law-abiding soul and all that that implied still rankled, and this behaviour was like banging on a bruise.

We locked up what, unless the price should prove quite fantastic, was virtually *our* house and went towards the car.

Nancy gave me an opening. "Why on earth," she asked, "didn't that booby Kenyon bring us here yesterday?"

"I can't say for certain," I said, "but I'd surmise that he thought we might not pass muster in Mrs. Bulmer's eyes. She's a very domineering, difficult old woman. I may tell you that it took me quite an effort to smooth her down."

That bolt missed its mark entirely. Nancy said, "If she's all that difficult she might change her mind. We should clinch it at once. Why on earth didn't you ask her how much she wanted. It sounds the rational thing to do. After all, she wants to *sell* the house."

"I don't think she does; she's sentimental about it. She visits it almost every day."

"She must be senile! And I'll tell you one thing; if we do buy it and live in it, I don't want her dropping in to see if that table's scrubbed et cetera. She sounds capable of it."

"You need not fear that. She has manners." I told her what Mrs. Bulmer, of whom I was now, in retrospect, quite fond, had said.

I don't think Nancy was giving me her attention, for the second I stopped speaking, she said, "Listen, I've worked out the best way to go to work. I'll drive home; you stay here and see Kenyon first thing in the morning and come home by train. I'll let the office know. Nail him down; pay a deposit. Have you your chequebook? To do a thing personally is always better and more satisfactory than a lot of writing."

Like most of her pronouncements this was right in principle and since the alternative was that she should stay and I should go and collect the boys, straight from the corruptive influence of forty-eight hours in Benjy's company, cajole them to bed, get them up, make breakfast, prod them off to school, I said that I thought it was a good idea.

I was in Kenyon's office before he was, in the morning; and when he came in his face assumed a complacent look; he imagined that I had had second thoughts about the bijou residence. I disillusioned him, telling him that we had stumbled by chance upon a house, just what we were looking for, the property of a Mrs. Bulmer, and, I was given to understand, on his books.

"Oh yes," he said. "Very pleasant little property indeed." He gave me a funny, I thought guilty, look. I felt like asking why he hadn't taken us there yesterday instead of wasting our time: but if we were to do business there was no point in poisoning our relationship at the start. And in effect he answered the unasked question.

"I didn't think of it," he said. "Freudian forgetfulness, if you like. It's a bit off the map and I worked on it, way back, but I got sick of it. I'd take people there on a fine day and they'd like it, then they'd go again, in bad weather, and call off. Or they'd go in the village—about the only really ugly one around here. You didn't go into the village?"

"No. As I told you, we were driving along and my wife . . ."

"Ah, here it is," he said, producing from a heap of papers in which he had been scrabbling, a mimeographed sheet, similar to those he had sent us in reply to our inquiry, but old, ragged, and yellowed about the edges. He didn't hand it to me, but in a flat, automatic voice ran through the particulars, such and such rooms, so many feet by so many; so much ground. "And a bargain at the price," he said. "Three thousand five hundred."

But I had cultivated the useful art of reading upside down; Sheep Hill House had gone on the market for five thousand, in typescript. In ink it had been marked down to four; in pencil down to three; in smudgy ball-point pen, two thousand four hundred. I didn't in the least resent his trying to get three thousand five hundred; I could afford it, and at that price the place was dirt cheap. But I wondered why the house was still for sale, and why the price had suffered such a steady reduction.

"I remember now; I knew there was something that made for difficulties. Some old furniture, not antique, just big old stuff which Mr. Bulmer's aunt had expressed a wish should remain in the house. That puts people off—some people anyway. I remember at one point I told Mr. Bulmer to put the stuff on the bonfire; I even offered to dispose of it for him. But apparently he'd promised his aunt. Sentiment, you know. And after all, whether the house sells or not makes no difference to him; she left him a packet all right."

He looked at me and misinterpreted my expression.

"You're not obliged to keep the rubbish. I've pointed that out to clients before. *You* didn't promise anything. All *you'd* have to do is pay what he's asking, twenty pounds if I remember right; and you'd have firewood for the winter."

I didn't speak.

"I tell you what I'll do. Mr. Bulmer would agree, I'm sure. Say three thousand five hundred, *inclusive*."

My mind was working like a computer operated by a madman. Out came a statement of sheer incredulity; the thing just wasn't possible. I'd never in all my life seen or talked to anyone more real than Mrs. Bulmer. Then, snapping into place, evidence on the other side, "my present limited accommodation," "one becomes attached," "have no fear that I shall always be on your doorstep." And then there emerged another, quite vital fact; I must be very careful; it would never do to start my career in Charrington with a reputation for seeing things that weren't there.

"That's a fair offer," I managed to say. "But of course about the furniture I must consult my wife. It's her domain, after all."

For a second his jaunty, salesman's face took on a resigned look, but it had recovered by the time he'd pushed the paper a little to one side.

"Naturally," he said "Excuse me." He lifted the telephone which had begun to scream.

"I'll get in touch with you," I said and blundered out of the office.

Now I am indeed in a dilemma. What am I going to tell Nancy? The truth? And she, with her complete disbelief in anything that can't be scientifically explained, will think my brain is affected. If there were only Nancy and I, I'd say nothing, go ahead and buy the house; Mrs. Bulmer as good as gave me her word, and if some time in the future Nancy did or said something that proved that she was unsuitable and provoked retaliative action, well, a meeting face to face with Mrs. Bulmer would do her no harm at all. But there are the boys; Edward I don't worry about, he's his mother's son; but suppose Peter . . . No, that is unthinkable.

My right hand felt cold and heavy and as though it didn't belong to me.

Nancy's quite capable of believing that I made up this story because I really preferred the bijou residence and daren't say so.

Nancy despises me and I don't think I'm quite as fond of her as I was on Saturday.

How happily we set out on Friday.

I have extra-sensory-perception. And I may well be about to have a stroke.